Noah's Lark

AMI Family Series

DANA L. BROWN

Published by:
Southern Yellow Pine (SYP) Publishing
4351 Natural Bridge Rd.
Tallahassee, FL 32305

www.syppublishing.com

This is a work of fiction. Names, characters, places, and events that occur either are the products of the author's imagination or are used fictitiously. Any resemblance to actual persons, places, or events is purely coincidental.

The contents and opinions expressed in this book do not necessarily reflect the views and opinions of Southern Yellow Pine Publishing, nor does the mention of brands or trade names constitute endorsement.

ISBN-13: 978-1-59616-109-2
ISBN-13 ePub: 978-1-59616-110-8
LCCN: 2020935505

Printed in the United States of America
First Edition
March 2020

Dedication

This book is about family and especially the bond between siblings. Just as Noah looks up to his big brother, Nick, I look up to my big brother, Tom. He's exactly five years and one day older than I am, and he's the only person who's known me my entire life. He's shared his birth month, his toys, and his heart with me for more years than I want to divulge, and I love him in the way only a little sister can. There hasn't been a day in my life when I didn't know he was there for me, and for that I'll be forever grateful.

(And I'm really sorry for pulling the eye off his teddy bear when I was four. *Really sorry*.)

Books by Dana L. Brown

The AMI Series

Lottie Loser
Call Me Charlotte
The Greysons

The AMI Family Series

Noah's Lark
Knot for Love (coming soon)

Prologue

Mermaids were dancing around the boat when the incessant pounding began. His mind still out to sea, the first thought was a problem with the engine, but as consciousness brought him back to reality, Noah realized the pounding was coming from the front door of his dad's marina.

Pulling on a pair of jeans, he stepped into the darkness of the living area and wondered why someone was so insistent on getting their attention in the middle of the night. Taking a quick glance at the clock in the kitchen, he saw that it was only four fifteen in the morning, and again he questioned what was going on.

The door to Pop's room was still closed, but Noah worked his way through the darkness before deciding if he even wanted to know who was on the other side of the pounding. His brother Nick was in the process of leaving his job as a Special Agent with the FBI because he'd been shot in his own home by a young man he'd put in prison. For that reason alone, Noah hesitated.

But when he heard the cry on the other side of the door, it not only hit him in the gut, it marked his heart.

"Nick, please, let me in," came the sobs. "It's Stella, Nick, please, I need you." Noah opened the door just as supermodel Stella Harper threw herself into his arms. It was obvious to him that in the darkness Stella mistook him for his big brother, the brother who had saved her from her stalker Adam Jennings, but at that minute, as he held the gorgeous sobbing girl in his arms, all he knew was she felt good. She felt damn good.

Once the beauty in his arms stopped weeping and was trying to catch her breath, Noah pulled gently away so she could see that it wasn't his brother who had been holding her and rubbing her back.

"Noah?" she questioned, moving out of arms reach. "Oh my gosh, I'm so embarrassed! Why didn't you stop me?"

Good question, he thought. Maybe because she had thrown herself at him without even considering that he wasn't Nick. Or maybe it was because it felt good to be needed by a woman, or maybe it was because the one woman in the world he had ever truly loved had just told him she was marrying his brother in two days. Noah wasn't sure of the reason, maybe it was a combination of all three, but standing there bare chested, wearing nothing but a pair of low-slung jeans, he knew he needed to tell her something.

"Because you needed help, Stella," he answered truthfully, "and it's what we Greyson men do."

He reached out and took her hand but didn't pull her in any closer. "Now why don't you tell me what's going on and why you came to Anna Maria Island before the crack of dawn."

"Would it be alright if I sat down?" Stella questioned. "I'm not feeling so good."

Noah led her to the couch and then went to the refrigerator to get her a bottle of water. After unscrewing the lid and handing her the bottle, he sat down beside her. "Now tell me what's wrong and how I can help?"

Stella took a big gulp of the water, and the tears started again. "It's Adam, Noah," she said with a shaky voice. "He was beat up in prison, but the guards found him before it was too late. Anyway, he's in the hospital, but it doesn't look good. And I feel like it's my fault. This whole mess has always been because of me." And with that, the sobbing started again.

Noah let her cry, patting her back with one thought in his mind. *What would Nick do?*

1

Now

Noah Greyson was not a man given to emotional outbursts, but when the minister said the words, "Should anyone here have just cause why this couple should not be joined in Holy matrimony, speak now or forever hold your peace," he almost lost it. But stoically, he kept smiling, his hands clamped and rigid at his sides, as his brother married the woman of their dreams. Lottie had always been Nick's girl. He'd even said those exact words to her, but that didn't mean he didn't want her, too. True, he'd never made a play for her, even after she'd come back to the island after college, but it wasn't like he hadn't thought about it. Nick was his big brother and his best friend, and there was an unwritten rule that you didn't go after a friend's girl, even if that friend was too pigheaded to go after her himself.

Instead, Noah had stood back, watching Nick and Lottie mess up their chances after high school, and then again this summer, but now here they were, holding hands and saying vows before God, while his heart was being ripped out of his chest. His sister Maya gave his arm a squeeze to let him know she was there and understood, and it helped, just not enough.

And like that, the "I dos," had been said, and the girl he'd loved since childhood, Lottie Luce, was now officially Charlotte Greyson, his brother's wife.

"Congratulations big brother," he said, slapping Nick on the back hard enough to force him to stop kissing his bride. "It's been a long time coming, but you finally got the girl, and no one deserves it more." The strangest part was that he meant it.

Charlotte was blushing when he pulled her into a hug and said, "I really am happy for you, Lottie." When she relaxed and hugged him back, he let his mind wander for just a moment before they were pulled apart by people wanting to congratulate the happy couple. What if he had been the groom and the slight roundness of her belly was his child growing inside of her? It was a fantasy that he'd allowed himself to have before, but he knew it was one he could never have again.

Scrubbing his hands over his face, he decided that he needed to get through this weekend with his mom, and then the only thing that would put his life back on track was a double shot of Patrón and getting laid. There was something about good tequila and a soft woman that could really make a man forget his troubles. And forgetting was exactly what he planned to do.

2
Then

Noah woke up with an upset stomach. Okay, maybe "woke up" was stretching it because he had never really gone to sleep, but his stomach hurt, and to be honest, his heart hurt even more. He loved his dad, and he liked living at the marina, but why did his mom have to pack him, and his sister and brother up in the middle of the school year and ship them back here? Didn't she care for them at all?

Noah Greyson was nine years old, the youngest of the three Greyson kids. His brother Nick was ten, and his sister Maya was thirteen, but for some reason the move from New York City wasn't bothering them like it was him. Maybe it was because Maya had lived here until she was six, and Nick made friends easily enough that it wasn't such a big deal for them, but Noah was different, even though he was trying to hide it.

"Rise and shine," Pop said, turning on the light in the boy's room. "Today's the first day at your new school, and you don't want to be late." Noah could hear Maya singing with the radio in her room, and he knew she was excited about the day, Nick got up with a smile on his face so Noah pasted a smile on his face too, even though happy was the last word he could think of to describe his mood.

How could Mom choose Hudson over us? he thought for the millionth time. Then letting out a big sigh, he knew the answer was still the same. His mom, their mom, liked bright lights and big cities, and the idea of traveling to far off glamorous places was stronger than her desire to be a mother.

"I made your favorite," Pop told Noah as he ruffled his hair. "Pancakes and bacon, extra crisp!"

Noah knew how happy Pop was to have his kids home, so he nodded and did his best to eat without anyone catching on to his unhappiness, but when he looked up, Nick was staring at him, and he knew the jig was up.

Instead of saying anything, or teasing him likes brothers do, Nick went back to eating, but he looked at Noah long enough to say, "I'm a little nervous about today; I'm sure glad I've got you to walk into school with."

And just like that, Noah felt better. Nick wasn't just his brother, he was his best friend, and in his heart, Noah knew that Nick was there for him and would always have his back.

As soon as breakfast was over, and his dishes rinsed and in the dishwasher, one of the few rules Pop insisted on, Noah went back to his room and got dressed. The dress code on Anna Maria Island was much more relaxed than in New York City, but Noah still carefully selected his clothes for that first day. Shorts, with just enough fray to look cool, a Coldplay T-shirt, and a pair of Birkenstocks, and his outfit was complete. He ran a little gel in his dirty blond hair and looked in the mirror.

"Okay, Greyson," he said out loud. "It's time to bring a little New York City to AMI." He was practicing his smile when he looked up and there stood Nick.

"Just be yourself, Noah." Nick encouraged. "You've always had lots of friends, and that isn't going to change. But if for some reason you feel out of place, find me at recess and we'll hang out. Okay?"

Noah looked at his brother and nodded. Grabbing their backpacks, the boys walked out together. Brothers by blood; best friends by choice.

3
Then

A home and a family of his own had been his one desire from the moment he'd met Elizabeth Andrews, but having to raise their kids by himself had never entered his mind. But now Nicholas Greyson was doing just that, and every day he worried that he wasn't doing it well enough. It had only been a week since he had gone to New York City and picked up his three children from the home of their mother and stepfather. Now they were living permanently with him at his marina on Anna Maria Island, Florida.

Today had been their first day of school since moving back to Florida, and Nicholas, or Pop to his kids, was waiting anxiously to hear about their day. At thirteen, Maya was a social butterfly and had already made friends with other girls in the neighborhood, but Nick and Noah, who were a year age, had each other and didn't seem in any hurry to meet new people. Nicholas was especially worried about Noah, because he'd been little more than a baby when his mother had whisked him off to New York City. Of his three kids, he knew that Noah was suffering the most from the move, but he didn't know how to make it better.

That's why on that first day after school, he had been thrilled when his sons came home with two new friends, confidant that their dad would be okay with it. After introducing himself and offering the girls a drink, he watched his boys interact with the two. He knew right then that the little girl with red curly hair would play an important part in his sons' futures. He didn't know why he felt that way; it was what his Aunt Barb would have called a *God wink,* but he knew it would happen. He just didn't know how.

4
Now

Once Nick and Charlotte had left for their honeymoon, Noah was able to relax and enjoy the time with his family. It had been twenty years since he'd been in a room with his mom and dad, and he found that he liked it. Now that everyone knew about Elizabeth's scleroderma, and that it was health concerns that had caused her to make up the story about her new husband wanting to travel and the kids being better off with their dad, there seemed to be a peace within the family that had been missing for all those years.

Noah watched his mother, her frail body draped in a pink satin caftan, holding court over the gathering, but he was okay with it. For the first time in a long time he was finally able to move past thinking he was the cause of his parents' divorce, and it felt really good. He worried a lot about his dad, but when he looked over at him, Pop was laughing along with everyone else, and his face was that of a man content with his life, and not one still feeling the pain of unrequited love. *Maybe there's hope for me after all*, he thought.

They cut the evening short when Elizabeth started to nod off, and her current husband, Gus, insisted it was time for her to go to bed. Noah and Pop went back across the hall to spend another night in the neighbor's apartment, and Maya and her family stayed in the magnificent Park Avenue apartment with their mom. Early the next morning, Pop and Maya's husband Dimitri were taking the twins and flying back to Florida, leaving Maya and him alone to become reacquainted with their mother. He fell asleep trying to decide if that thought was thrilling or terrifying.

The day started innocently enough. Pop, Dimi, and the twins left before the others were up, and now Noah and Maya were left alone with their mom.

"Come sit by me, Noah," his mother said, patting the chair beside her. "Let's get you some breakfast, and you can tell me all about what's going on in your life."

Her smile was so sincere that he wasn't prepared for what she said next. "You know Charlotte wasn't the right girl for you, don't you, dear? You're much too soft-hearted for a girl with her spirit."

He would have gotten up and left the apartment right then, but Maya chose that moment to make her entrance.

"Good morning," she said brightly. "There's nothing like waking up overlooking Central Park to start your day out right, is there? You sleep okay, Noah?"

Maybe it was the scowl on his face or the way he was clenching and unclenching his fists that got her attention, but Maya quickly realized that her brother was pissed. Really pissed. She hadn't been given the nickname Mama Bear for nothing, so immediately, she started damage control.

"What's wrong?" she questioned her brother. When he didn't answer she turned to her mother. "Noah's a morning person and not easily riled-up. What happened to upset him?"

By now Noah had started to calm down, but Maya was getting worked up. She glared at her mother who casually replied, "I was telling Noah that Charlotte wasn't the right woman for him, and he got that look on his face. I'm his mother; I just want the best for him."

Maya looked like she could chomp down on rocks and spit them into pebbles, but all of a sudden, Noah started to laugh.

"You're right, Mom," he told her. "Charlotte was never the right woman for me, but how you even knew about my feelings is what I'm upset about. So tell me," he said looking in his sister's direction, "who spilled the beans?"

"No one had to tell me, Noah," Elizabeth answered. "It was all over your face every time you looked Charlotte's way. She's a wonderful girl, and I already love her, but she would never have been right for you."

9

She looked so sincere that Noah just shook his head. Taking his mother's hand, he looked her way and smiled. "I appreciate your concern for my welfare, Mom. I truly do, but talking about my love life is not a conversation we're ever going to have again. Are we clear?"

Elizbeth looked like she was about to cry, but she squeezed her son's hand and smiled. "I just want you to be happy," she was finally able to say.

Noah squeezed back and replied, "me too."

5
Now

They'd had a great evening when Nick and Charlotte had come for dinner on the last night of their honeymoon, and Noah had done his best to man up to the situation. The first thing he'd noticed when the newlyweds walked in was the whisker burn on Lottie's face, and it was like a punch to the gut. But he pulled her into a bear hug and said, "Marriage looks good on you, Lottie." He could see the blush on her face, so he winked, hoping to let her know everything was going to be okay between them.

Now it was Friday morning, and Nick and Lottie were getting ready to head home to Anna Maria Island to start their life together. Noah looked around the dining room of his mom's spectacular Park Avenue apartment, seeing the happy look on the faces of his family, and realized how much he had missed this growing up. Yes, his dad had been the best parent any kid could have asked for, and he dearly loved his sister and brother, but not having his mom in his life had left a big hole in his heart. Now that hole was beginning to fill.

Charlotte and his mom got up from the table and headed to the bedroom, and Maya went in to call Dimi and the twins, leaving him the opportunity to tell Nick about his strange middle of the night visit from Stella Harper. Noah could see the concern on Nick's face, wondering why Charlotte wanted to see their mother privately, but he knew this might be his only opportunity to get his brother alone.

"Uh, could I talk with you a minute, Nick?" Noah asked.

"Sure, what's up?" Nick replied.

"Right before we left for New York, Stella came to the marina looking for you." Noah said, running his hand through his dirty blond hair.

"What in the world was Stella doing at the marina?" Nick asked. "The only time she came there was right after I was released from the hospital."

Noah told his brother the story about Adam Jennings being badly beaten in prison, and that Stella thought it had something to do with her. He could tell that Nick wasn't happy that he was staying in contact with Stella, but at this point he wasn't about to turn his back on her.

"Stella's a good kid, Noah, and as innocent as they come. All those years of being dragged around to modeling gigs and Adam stalking her have really done a number on her head. Maybe someone else would be better suited to be her comforter?"

"Don't worry about Stella, big brother, just take care of your wife." Noah patted Nick's back and said, "I'm serious, Nick. Take good care of Lottie."

Nick gave his brother a hug and told him, "I will, Noah, you can count on that."

When Noah turned around, he saw a beautiful sight before him. His mom and his sister were holding hands and waiting for him to join them. For the past twenty years he'd thought so many times of what having his family together would be like, and now he knew. His parents seemed to have reached an understanding, and he had his mother in his life again. And for now, that was going to be enough.

***

It was good to be home, Noah thought, as he stepped inside the marina. Pop and Nick had been there when he and Maya had walked down the gangplank, and even though he'd enjoyed the lunch at Stavros with Dimi and the twins, he was ready to get his life back. Whatever that was.

Plopping down on his bed, Noah closed his eyes and thought about the past few days. They'd been better than he would ever have expected, but now it was time to move forward. The images he'd had about a double shot of tequila and a soft woman lying beside him were as vivid in his mind as a watercolor on canvas, and he smiled thinking about them. He'd never had a problem finding a beautiful woman to spend time with, and tequila? That wouldn't be a problem either.

12

But not tonight because Pop had invited Nick and Lottie over for dinner, and it would seem like he was running away from them if he wasn't there. So instead, he unpacked and went outside to check *The Lark*. He hadn't been out on the open water in weeks, and if he was going to get back his life, it was the first place to start.

It was hard to keep a grin off his face when Noah approached his slip. His life as a charter boat captain had never even entered his thoughts as a kid, but that changed when he met Chester.

6

Then

Noah sat on the deck, a cold can of Coke in his hand, his high school diploma proudly displayed on his dresser, and thought about his future. Unlike his brother Nick, who had just finished his first year at the University of Florida, Noah had no idea what he wanted to do with his life. He was a good student and had been accepted into college. What to major in was still the question of the day.

"Hey, Noah," his dad called from the dock, "Chester wants to talk with you a minute."

Chester Davis was one of his dad's oldest friends and customers. He had a Carolina custom made boat that he'd taken both Greyson boys out fishing on numerous times, so as Noah walked down to the dock his thoughts quickly changed to fun, and away from what he was going to do with his future.

Chester had been a career navy man and liked to give the impression of being tough. But Noah knew that in reality Chester was a softy and what Pop called, "The salt of the earth." His wife, Lucy, had been a back-up singer for some rock and roll group when he'd met her, so in her honor he named his boat, *The Lark.* Lucy had been his first mate and co-captain until her health started to fail. Now Chester only took a few charters a month, but a day never passed by without him coming down to check on *The Lark.*

But a fishing trip was not what Chester was thinking about today. Being a man of few words, he immediately told Noah what he had in mind.

"My deck hand up and quit this morning," Chester said in his gruff and raspy voice. "I came down to see if you're interested in the job. I already asked your Pop, and he said it's up to you."

Noah looked at his dad and then back at Chester, not really sure how to answer. He had planned to help out at the marina this summer, but if being a deck hand would mean being out on the open water, he was in.

Chester could see the gears grinding in Noah's mind so he added, "I'll pay you a stipend, but most of what you'll get paid in is experience. Being a deck hand is hard work, but you'll get to visit some pretty sweet ports, as well as learn how to run a boat. So what do you say; do we have a deal?"

Noah shook the hand that was extended his way, and said, "Yes, sir, we sure do."

"Today's your last day of freedom," Chester chuckled, "I'll see you back here tomorrow at zero four hundred hours. And don't stay out all night with some filly. You're going to need your strength."

Noah gulped and nodded. Four in the morning was still the middle of the night as far as he was concerned, plus he already had a date set with a brunette he'd met at Two Scoops the day before. She was soft in all the right places, just the way he liked a girl to be, and he'd hoped to get at least past first base with her. But when he looked at his new boss, he knew his plans for any back-seat activities were going to have to be postponed.

"Bright and early, "Chester told him again. "And don't let me down."

7
Now

He ran his hands over the silky-smooth wood of the hull; caressing it as if it were a beautiful woman. Noah loved his boat and most years would have spent the entire summer on her, but when Nick was shot, it had changed everything. Pop's marina gave him a safe place to store his prize possession when he was on land, and there was always a kid around happy to swab the decks and keep an eye on things for him, but now he was restless to get back out to sea.

"She's still a beauty," Pop said walking up beside him, a beer in each hand.

"Even after all these years, I have to pinch myself sometimes to believe this is all real," Noah said as he accepted one of the beers from his pop and took a long drink. "But now that Nick's on the mend, I think it's time I go back to work and earn my keep."

Pop nodded, knowing how much his youngest son was struggling, but proud of the man he'd become. "You and *The Lark* always have a home here; you know that right, son?" Pop asked. "Maybe someday you'll be tired of life on the water, and you'll want to come back here and put down roots. When that day comes, I'd be pleased to have you for a partner."

Elizabeth had been right about her youngest son, he was a kindhearted man, so it was no surprise to his father when the hand he extended to Noah for a shake, pulled him in for a hug. "I appreciate that, Pop, and maybe someday I'll take you up on it, but for now, I need some time to think, and to do that I have to get away from the island."

Pop didn't answer; he didn't have to. Both Greyson men, father and son knew how it felt to be in love with a woman you couldn't have, and talking about it wasn't going to change things. Sometimes you had to work through heartache in your own way, and if getting back out to sea would help Noah heal, his dad was all for it.

Pop walked back to the house to start working on dinner, and Noah gave his boat a good inspection. When he climbed aboard, he was filled with the same excitement that he'd felt when he was eighteen. The cabin wasn't large, but it was big enough to hold a few guests. The galley and head were small but serviceable, and the bedroom was perfect for nights when Noah invited company onboard. Female company that is.

He shook his head and thought about all those years he'd lain in that bed, thinking about making love to Lottie, while *The Lark* swayed with the gentle rhythm of the waves, but he realized now that she would never have thought it was romantic. It wasn't that she had too much spirit for him but that she was out of his class. He'd heard her tell Maya about the sunglasses she'd bought at Tiffany for fuck's sake! Sunglasses that you could buy at Island Bazaar for under ten bucks, and she'd bought hers at a fancy jewelry store.

Satisfied that everything was ready for his departure, Noah walked back up to the house with his thoughts on finding an upcoming fishing competition. He was barely inside when he looked out the door and saw Lottie sitting outside in her bright red Grand Prix.

"Hey Shortcake!" Noah yelled through the doorway, still using his childhood nickname for her. "Are you coming in to greet your favorite brother-in-law or are you going to sit out there and daydream?"

She slid out of the car and was about to give him a saucy retort and a hug when a big, strong body stepped between them.

"Hands off my woman, little brother," Nick told him coming out of the kitchen. "Those days are over."

8
Then

"Is Lottie your girlfriend?" Noah asked his brother one day a few months after they had moved back to Anna Maria Island.

"What do you mean by girlfriend?" Nick questioned. "She's a girl and we're friends; is that what you mean?"

"No, you dummy," Noah laughed as he threw a pillow across the room. "Is she your *girlfriend;* like do you hold hands and kiss her and stuff?"

Nick threw back the pillow and rolled his eyes. "Where do you come up with this stuff, Noah? That's just gross. Kissing a girl, yuck!"

Noah pulled the pillow over his face so that Nick wouldn't see how embarrassed he was. What was wrong with wanting to kiss a girl? He'd seen it happen in movies, and it didn't look so bad. And kissing Lottie? He was sure he'd like that.

"Come on," Nick said, trying to change the subject. "Let's swim out to the platform. I'll give you a ten second head start, and I'll still beat you!"

Noah jumped off the bed and ran through the house. Nick always beat him at swimming out to the platform, but this time he was determined to be the winner. Diving into the warm Gulf of Mexico water, still in his cut-off jeans and a T-shirt, all thoughts of Lottie Luce were gone. But just like beating his brother in a race to the platform, those thoughts were there in the back of his mind, waiting for another day to surface.

9

Now

The dinner with Nick and Lottie was nice, but Noah couldn't help but feel envious, especially when he saw the way they looked at each other. And now Pop was spending time with Shelly Bert, Nick's nurse from his time in the hospital, making Noah feel all the more alone.

As soon as Nick and Lottie said their goodnights and her car was out of sight, Noah grabbed his keys and said he was going to the Crab Shack. He'd already had a couple beers, so it probably wasn't the night for tequila, but a few Cigar City Brewing Company beers sounded about right.

It was still early when he got to the Shack, but that meant he'd find a good seat at the bar so he could keep an eye on the door. There were several local ladies who he'd enjoyed spending time with in the past, and he was hoping one of them would stop by tonight for a glass of wine and a good time. Of course, how good would depend on them. If there was one thing Noah Greyson didn't do, it was force himself on a woman. But then again, he'd never had to.

After three beers and no lovelies in sight, Noah ordered some crab cake bites and moved to a booth. At this point he saw his chances for companionship for the night diminish, and he wanted to eat and sulk in private.

When the food arrived, it brought back the memory of the night he had danced here with Lottie, Nick watching with a jealous scowl on his face. It was the same night that she'd had too much to drink and done a partial striptease in front of them, and the only time he'd had an up close and personal view of her voluptuous curves. He'd harassed Nick, knowing how badly his brother wanted the gorgeous redhead, but the sight of Lottie in the sheer lace bra and panties had about been his own undoing.

The crab cakes lost their appeal, but Noah ate them because he needed something in his stomach besides beer. He even ordered a Coke, hoping some caffeine in his system would help and took a large drink from the icy can to cool himself down. "Get a grip, Greyson," he said out loud, and then punched in the number of the one woman he thought might want to talk with him.

"Hi, this is Stella," the recording began. "Leave me a message and I'll call you back."

"Fuck!" Noah exclaimed, slamming the phone down on the table. He only wanted to talk with a woman, any woman to get his mind off Lottie, but apparently tonight wasn't going to be his night. It wasn't as if he had any interest that way in Stella. She was only a kid and way too skinny for his taste, but at least she was a female, and he liked talking to her.

Taking the last drink of his Coke, he slapped some money on the table and was about to call it a night when Lindsey Brothers slipped into the seat beside him. "Hey handsome," she said in her soft and sultry voice. "Where've you been keeping yourself?"

Noah looked into her big blue eyes and could feel his body stir. Lindsey was always up for some no strings attached activity, and that was just what the doctor ordered tonight. But as he was about to respond to her question, his phone started playing his latest country song ringtone. He wouldn't have even looked to see who the caller was, but after the call saying Nick had been shot, he never ignored one.

Lindsey was stroking his thigh, fueling the fire he was already feeling, when the name on the caller ID registered. Hitting the green button to accept the call, he moved Lindsey's hand from his leg and said, "Hey Stella."

Once she'd heard Noah say another woman's name, Lindsey huffed, puffed, and flipped her long blonde streaked curls, making a noisy exit from the booth. Noah tried to keep the frustration out of his voice, but damn, Lindsey Brothers was definitely good for what ailed a man. But he'd called Stella because he was lonely, and he couldn't be rude now that she'd called him back.

"Sorry I missed your call," Stella told him, "I was at some political thing with my parents, and they have a big rule about no cell phones in view when my mom's on display."

Noah could hear the sadness in her voice, and it tugged at his heart. Stella Harper was not only the daughter of a United States Senator; she had been the Sports Illustrated Swimsuit cover model two years in a row and was considered one of the world's top models. But despite all the notoriety, she was really a lonely young girl.

"It's fine," he responded, feeling guilt at only calling her because he was lonely himself. His life was paradise compared to what Stella had lived through, and using her to boost his ego made him feel terrible.

Lindsey had already moved on to a new playmate, so Noah slipped out of the bar and talked to Stella as he walked down the beach. Seeing that he was close to Lottie's pink cottage, he found a bench and sat down. "I wanted to let you know that Nick is now officially a married man, and that I'm back from New York. You know, in case you needed to talk or anything."

"I'm happy for Nick; I really am," Stella told him. "The whole time he was protecting me all he talked about was Lottie and how he'd messed up with her. It was so sweet."

"*Sweet?*" Noah laughed. "You thought that was sweet? I call it pathetic. He fu—, I mean fouled up big time, and he deserved what he got. Sweet, please."

Noah could hear her relax as they talked, and it made him feel good. Stella needed a friend, not someone else trying to run her life, and that's exactly what he wanted to be. She might be one of the world's most beautiful women, but inside she was a lost little girl who needed a champion. Normally that was his brother's department, but for the first time, Noah was ready to step-up to the plate.

"Tell me about your mom's big event," Noah teased. "If I'd have been there who would we have made fun of behind their back?"

"Noah Greyson, you are so bad," she laughed, "but to be honest, there would have been several."

And like that, both of their nights looked rosier.

10
Now

By the time they ended the call, the effects of the beer had worn off. Noah looked at his watch and realized he'd been talking with Stella for over an hour, something he hadn't done since high school. He chuckled to himself, and he climbed in his truck, thinking about how nice it had been to have a conversation with a woman. No flirting, no innuendos or suggestive banter, just down to earth everyday conversation.

But those thoughts came to an abrupt halt when he heard pounding on the window and realized that Lindsey was trying to get inside.

"Hey cowboy, unlock the door and let me in," she said, flashing him a big smile.

Noah scrubbed his hands over his face, not sure what to do. There was still plenty of moonlight left, and the look Lindsey was giving him let him know exactly what she was after. The thing was, it had been a long day, and now he really wanted to go to bed. Alone. But he'd already turned Lindsey down once tonight, and the ache in his groin was telling him not to be a fool.

Lindsey wasn't very tall, so as she maneuvered herself into the passenger seat of the pickup, her tight jean skirt rode high on her thighs, giving Noah a generous glance at her tiny satin panties. If he'd had any doubts about where this night was headed, they were left behind on the beach.

"Where to?" he asked, trying to at least act like a gentleman.

Lindsey scooted beside him and placed her hand on his arm.

"Surprise me," she whispered in his ear, as she let her fingers slowly walk down his chest to the very visible bulge in his jeans.

"Lindsey," Noah said, trying to keep his voice steady. "I can take you home, or I can take you here, but it's not going to take long. It's your choice."

After making sure no one else was in the parking lot, Lindsey reached for his zipper without ever taking her eyes off him. Freeing him from the denim, she stroked his silky length and then took him into her mouth.

Noah was right, it didn't take long, and quickly his hands were threaded in her curls as he did his best to stay quiet. When he knew he was close he told her to stop, but Lindsey continued until he emptied himself in her mouth.

Noah Greyson had been with a lot of women, and he'd never been ashamed of that fact until tonight. He'd used Lindsey in the most intimate way, and now he felt like an ass. He loved women, he loved making love to women, but he'd treated her like a whore, and that was making him sick inside, especially because he could tell that she was expecting more, and he didn't have anything left to give her.

Fastening his jeans, he uttered some words about calling her, leaving Lindsey looking angry and confused. "I guess I'll see you around," she said sarcastically and slid out of the truck and slammed the door.

Noah watched to make sure she made it to her car safely, and when she pulled away in a fury, he finally turned the key in the engine. When he got home, he entered the house quietly, not up to a talk with Pop about his night. His reputation with women was no secret to his family, but his dad had told him early on to make sure he treated every one he spent time with like a lady. And until tonight, he had.

Thankful that his dad was in bed, Noah let out a sigh of relief and headed to his own room. He felt like shit, but he needed some advice from someone whose eyes wouldn't reflect his shame. Grabbing his phone, he sent a quick text, mentally crossing his fingers that he wasn't interrupting something.

Is this a bad time?

No, but what's going on that you're texting me at this time of night?

Do you have any free time tomorrow? Alone?

23

I can meet you for lunch after I do a few things to get ready for class.

That works, just name the time and place.

Cortez Kitchen about 1:00pm?

See you then.

Is everything okay?

It will be, Nick, just as soon as The Lark and I get away from AMI.

11
Then

Noah loved working for Chester. They were only taking a couple of charters out each month, but he lived for his time on the open water. The fishing tournaments up and down the coast were a whole new way of life for him even though he'd been raised around boats and fisherman. That's why he'd made up his mind that when the summer ended, he wanted to stay on with Chester and *The Lark* and forget about college. Chester thought differently.

"I know this all seems a lot like playing pirate, son, but trust me it's not. Having you aboard this summer has taken a big load off my back. You've been damn fine help, but come September, you're going off to college just like you planned."

Noah was ready with his objections, but Chester held firm. "There's no negotiation here," he said. "You go to school and learn all that you can; then when you get home next summer, we'll talk again."

And that's exactly what he did. For the next two years, Noah Greyson lived the whole campus experience September through May, but the minute classes were over, he came home to Anna Maria Island and *The Lark*. When he graduated with an associate degree in Marine Technology, Chester rewarded him by making him the Captain of the boat they both loved.

"I don't know what to say," Noah smiled. "We can go back to the way things were, but you could give me a raise."

Chester was smiling from ear to ear as he slapped Noah on the back. "You've earned this, boy, and besides, I'm getting too old to keep captaining this boat. My girl needs a young man at her helm, and you're the one I want guiding her through the gulf waters. And as to that raise? I think you'll like my offer there, too."

12

Now

He found a table as far away as possible from other people enjoying the eclectic outdoor dining of the Cortez Kitchen and sat down. His stomach was doing somersaults at the idea of putting food in it, and he knew he was too wired for his usual beer. Opting instead for a Sprite, he told the waitress that someone was joining him, and he'd wait to order.

Noah was so deep in his thoughts, he almost jumped out of his seat when Nick tapped him on the shoulder.

"You scared the shit out of me," Noah said, his hand automatically covering his thumping heart.

Nick chuckled and pulled up a chair. "You did invite me, little brother," he said. "But I didn't mean to scare you. I guess whatever's going on with you really is a big deal."

The server chose that time to return and took their orders for blackened grouper sandwiches and onion rings. Noah held up his can to signify that he needed another Sprite, and Nick said that he'd have the same.

"So what's up, Noah?" Nick asked with concern. "You didn't even flirt with the waitress, and I've got to tell you, she's a cutie."

Noah put his head in his hands and said, "I want what you have, Nick."

"If by what I have you mean my wife…?" Nick questioned, just as Noah cut him off.

"Not your wife, Nick, I want your life. I'm tired of flirting with waitresses and having sex in parking lots. I want a real relationship with a real woman, but first I have to rectify a big mistake I made with one."

Nick waited until the server brought their drinks and moved on to another table before replying. "You've only been back from New York a day, Noah. What the fuck happened?"

That brought a much-needed smile to Noah's face. "I didn't think your wife let you use that word anymore," he teased his brother.

Nick gave him his very serious FBI glare and responded. "*My wife* doesn't police my language, but I don't use it around her out of respect."

And that was the problem. Noah hadn't been respectful to Lindsey, and it was tearing him apart.

The sigh that Noah released could have filled a balloon. He'd asked Nick here for advice, but now that he had his brother's undivided attention, he wasn't sure where to start.

"Last weekend was great," he began guardedly. "Having the whole family together for the first time in twenty years was special and memorable, but you have to know that watching you and Lottie say your marriage vows was hard for me."

Nick nodded and said, "Go on."

"I thought if I hooked up with someone, I'd be fine, get rid of some tension and you know, some of the other feelings I was having, but it didn't work out that way. I treated a woman with anything but respect, and I need to fix it."

"Is this someone you'd like to have a real relationship with or just one you used?"

"You're here to make me feel better, Nick, not worse." Noah growled. "But no, she's not someone I'd want anything permanent with. She's always been good for a few laughs, but I'm sure she sees other guys besides me."

"And does she know you're not looking for anything long term?"

The waitress sat down their food before Nick could say another word, giving Noah a short reprieve. "I think I'm going to need a beer," Noah told her.

Nick chimed in, "Make that two."

Both men took a long pull of the frosty brew put before them, and then Noah started in.

"Here's the bottom line," he said. "She gave me a blow job in the cab of my truck while we were parked outside the Crab Shack. I didn't even kiss her, Nick. I was exhausted and horny, and she offered what I was looking for, so I took it. Plain and simple, I took advantage of the situation, and now I need to fix it. And then fix my life."

For a few moments both men concentrated on the food before them as well as the issue. Nick put the last of his sandwich in his mouth, took a drink and said, "First thing you have to do is apologize. Then, you need to quit hanging out in bars if you mean what you say about wanting a partner and not just another roll in the hay."

Noah was about to object, but then he realized that Nick was right. "Apologizing may be the hardest part of that equation," he responded. "She was pretty mad. But I'll do it because it's the right thing to do. Then I'm taking off until I can get my head on straight."

"I get it, Noah, and Pop will, too. There's someone out there for you, but you may have to go out and find her. Now, are you going to eat that sandwich you've been picking at because the one room in the house my wife isn't good in is the kitchen. She bought grapefruit juice for heaven's sakes! Can you believe it?"

Noah passed his plate to his brother and gave him a grin. "You're rubbing salt in the wounds," he chuckled, but for the first time in days his heart felt lighter and more at ease. Now he had to go apologize to Lindsey and get *The Lark* ready for an adventure on the high seas. Or at least the gulf coast.

13
Now

Noah knew he was taking a chance showing up at Lindsey's door with a bouquet of flowers, but what he had to say needed to be said in person. He'd never thought of her as anything other than a good time, but he liked her, and couldn't leave until he straightened out this mess.

When Lindsey opened the door, she glared at him, but when she saw the flowers her face softened, and she invited him in.

"I thought you were all talk when you said you'd call me," she smiled, taking the flowers from his hands. "But this is way better than a call."

Lindsey Brothers was more than pretty; she was striking. Her long, naturally curly hair ran down her back like a waterfall and perfectly framed her cornflower blue eyes. At about five feet four she was almost a foot shorter than Noah, but she was filled out exactly the way he liked. As they stood there, he could see how her blouse strained to cover her more than ample chest, and her backside was every boy's wet dream. But she wasn't the woman of Noah's dreams, and he knew he had to tell her that.

Lindsey had her nose in the flowers, a smile of satisfaction covering her face.

"Uh, Lindsey," he began. "About the other night."

Before he could go further, she took his hand and looked sweetly into his face. "It's okay, Noah," she told him. "It was late and things happen."

Fuck! This was not the way he wanted this conversation to go. "Please let me finish," he said, letting go of her hand. "You're right, it was late, and I was tired, but that's no excuse for what happened. I like you Lindsey, and you're a beautiful woman, but I treated you badly and for that I'm sorry; I'm so sorry. We've had some fun together, but that's all it ever was. You understand that, right?"

Noah could see her face melting, but he stood quietly, waiting for her to say something.

"I guess deep down I knew that I was never special to you, but I thought I could change your mind."

"You are special Lindsey, and you need to find a man who knows that the minute he looks in your beautiful blue eyes. But never change yourself for a man, Lindsey. Promise me you'll remember that," Noah told her gently, moving towards the door.

"You make it sound like we'll never see each other again," she responded, the tears welling up in her eyes.

"I'm not saying never, but I need to get back to work and that means being gone for long stretches at a time. Anyway, I wanted to apologize for the other night and tell you face to face that as soon as I get some things together, I'll be heading out."

She couldn't reach his neck, so Lindsey put her arms around his waist and gave him a goodbye hug. "Be safe, Noah Greyson," she told him. "Thank you for the flowers and the apology. I've always known you as a bad boy, but now I realize that you're more than that; you're a good man."

Noah kissed her cheek, said goodbye, and pulled the front door closed. He breathed a big sigh of relief as he climbed in his truck and headed straight home to the one girl he could always count on, *The Lark*.

14
Then

For the next year Noah worked hard for Chester and became a real seaman. He learned everything there was to know about being the skipper of a charter boat, including how to navigate through the often-rough waters of the Gulf of Mexico with a cabin full of wannabe fisherman. Chester even started letting him plan trips to some fishing competitions; something he had never been involved in before.

Noah's twenty-first birthday fell on a Friday, and he had every intention of finding a girl and buying his first legal beer. But when he arrived back to the marina after a long day in the hot Florida sun, a surprise awaited him.

His sister Maya, her husband Dimi, their two-year-old twin daughters, Nikki and Steffi, his brother Nick, and Chester's wife Lucy were all there to greet him, blowing horns and clapping. Pop came in carrying a huge chocolate fudge cake with Chester following close behind. Everyone he loved was there. Everyone, that is, except Lottie.

Pop had just pulled Noah's favorite baby back ribs from the grill, and a big bowl of potato salad and a platter of corn on the cob were already on the table. Maya and Lucy filled glasses with ice and Pop's secret recipe lemonade, and everyone gave a toast to the birthday boy.

After dinner the group met in the living room for presents, cake, and ice cream. The gifts from his family were funny, as was the Greyson tradition, and then it was time for the one from Chester and Lucy. Noah could see that Chester looked nervous, and he worried that his friend was ill. But while he was thinking about Chester, the old sailor started giving a speech.

"You were the best deck hand I ever had," he started. "And when you became my first mate, I thought you'd found your place. But you surprised me, and when the time came for you to take over the helm, there were no surprises in how well you learned. I told you when I made you Captain that my girl needed a young person at the wheel, and I meant it. Me and Lucy are ready to see the world by land now, so this gift is from us. You've become like the son we never had, and we couldn't be prouder of you. Happy Birthday, Captain Greyson."

Noah was having a hard time holding back the tears, and he could see that his sister wasn't even trying. Pop had a huge smile on his face, and Nick was poised with a camera to capture Noah's expression when he opened the box Chester was offering.

What in the world could it be that would cause this much emotion? A captain's hat with his name on it? Or maybe a weekend cruise for just him and some friends? Whatever he thought it might be, Noah was not prepared for what he found inside the package.

"Congratulations," he read, "to the new owner of *The Lark,* Noah Christopher Greyson." Under the letter were legal papers naming him as the true new owner of the boat, and at this point, the tears were falling freely down his suntanned face.

"I don't know what to say," he stammered as both Chester and Lucy pulled him close.

"You say thank you, boy," Chester laughed. "And then you cut that fancy cake your Pop made.

At twenty-one years of age, Noah Greyson became the owner of the prettiest Carolina custom he'd ever seen. Chester had told him of the old sailor's superstition about changing the name on a boat, but Noah wasn't sure he believed in superstitions. None the less, for now, he continued to call her *The Lark.*

It was a few weeks later that he invited his family and friends over for a christening celebration. If Chester was concerned he didn't show it, but when Noah pulled the tarps off the side of the boat and passed out glasses of champagne instead of breaking the bottle against the bow, he put a big smile on his face and let out a huge sigh of relief.

"It is with great pride that I rechristen you, *The Lark,*" Noah beamed, looking at Chester and Lucy. "In honor of my dear friend, Chester Davis, and his beautiful songbird, Lucy."

The original lettering was still in place, and the name didn't change, but from that day forward, to anyone who knew him, she was known simply as *Noah's Lark.*

15

Now

As soon as he was home, Noah started looking for any upcoming fishing tournaments and found one about two weeks out in Louisiana. He knew it was a little late in the game to put together a team, but he entered anyway. There were always guys hanging around the wharfs who were anxious to be involved, so he entered his credit card number and hoped he was making a good decision.

Once that was taken care of, he headed to the docks to see what last minute details he needed to take care of on *The Lark*. Pop was already down there, working on an eighty-three-foot Ferretti pleasure boat, and he called for Noah to come aboard.

"She sure is a beauty," Pop said. "If I was a younger man I could go for a boat like this."

Noah slapped him on the back. "You're not that old, Pop," he teased. "Maybe you should grab that sweet Shelly and make all your dreams come true. Heck, there's even four cabins so we could take a family vacation."

"What is it with everyone trying to pair me up with Shelly? We've spent a little time together, but it's no big deal," Pop grumbled. "And besides, I spent enough years at sea. Now I have the best of both worlds. I can play at being a sailor but go home to my comfortable bed on land at night."

Noah's grin only made his dad growl more. "What?" he asked.

"Pop," he told his father. "Everyone can tell how much you like Shelly, and how much she likes you, so what are you waiting for? Because as you said yourself, you're not such a young man anymore."

"I'll show you old," Pop spat, and both men burst out laughing.

"I've entered a Cajun fishing competition in Louisiana, and as soon as *The Lark* is ready, I'm going to head out. Its only about an eleven-hour trip, but I plan to go slow and get my head on straight while it's just me, the water, and the sky." Noah said. "Is there anything here I need to do for you before I go?"

Pop shook his head. "The marina's in good shape, but I appreciate the offer. What you can do for me though is tell me why you're in such a rush to get away. I understand about Lottie, but that's nothing new. Is there something else I need to know about?"

Noah ran his hands through his sun-bleached hair, afraid to make eye contact with his dad. "I made a mistake Pop," he told him. "But it's been like a wake-up call. Hell, I'm thirty years old, and what have I done with my life? I sat on the deck when I was eighteen thinking about my future, and now I'm having those thoughts again."

"I understand those thoughts, Noah. I have them myself from time to time. All I need to know is that you're okay and you'll be careful." Pop paused, his voice cracking with emotion. "After what happened with Nick, I'll never stop needing to know that you kids are all right. As a parent, you think your job is done when your children grow up, but what a fool's thought that is."

"I'm not great, Pop, but I'm working on it, and I'll be careful; I promise you that." Noah put his arm around his dad, and together they made their way to *The Lark*.

16
Now

Less than a week later Noah climbed aboard *The Lark* and was underway. It was a beautiful Florida morning with big puffy clouds that resembled heads of cauliflower in the sky and soft cresting waves in the water. This was where he felt the most at peace, and he couldn't have held his smile back if he'd tried.

The evening before he'd called Stella to tell her he was leaving for a few weeks, and she told him about an upcoming modeling gig she had scheduled. She shared that Adam was still hospitalized, and even though she'd tried, they wouldn't allow her in to see him. They'd said their goodbyes with a promise to talk when they both got back, and Noah hung up, wishing once more he knew how to be a better friend to her. Maybe Nick had been right when he said she needed someone else to be her comforter, but he wasn't quite ready to step aside.

After a couple of hours, he cut the engine and threw out the anchor. It was too early for lunch and too early for a beer so he grabbed a bottle of icy cold water from the cooler and drank it down in one gulp. The newest Virgil Flowers novel by John Sandford was waiting on deck so he stripped off his shirt and settled into one of the lounge chairs.

The next thing he knew, the sun was beating down overhead, and the book was lying opened on his stomach. Giving his long body a stretch, he noticed how red his arms were and swore out loud. "Fuckin' rookie mistake," he said, maneuvering himself out of the chair.

His stomach was growling, letting him know it was past lunch time, and the water he'd drank seemed to have evaporated in the heat, but before he put anything in his stomach, he went in search of aloe and sunscreen. The spray was cool against his already burned face, but he continued spraying until all his uncovered skin was coated. Deciding he looked a little bit like a glazed ham, Noah put back on his shirt, wincing once or twice in discomfort.

Opening the cooler, he found a roast beef sandwich and a cold can of Coors Light, telling himself the beer would be like a painkiller for the sunburn. Instead of going back on deck, he ate his lunch in the cabin and decided it was time to move on.

The anchor up and the engine going, he took off and headed in the direction of Louisiana.

The afternoon skies were beautiful and the water was calm, but after so many weeks on land while Nick recuperated, Noah found that he missed having someone to talk to. This was a new development for him, and he wasn't sure if he liked it. The radio reception was iffy, so he tried the iTunes on his phone, but it wasn't much better. Soon he was approaching the Port of Pensacola and figured it was a good time to pull in for the night.

After a normal day on the water, Noah would stop at a port long enough to refuel, refill his supplies, and find a woman to share his bed for the night. After securing *The Lark* and making a deal with the kid who had topped off the tank to keep an eye on her for a few hours, he walked into the small harbor community, thinking about sex.

It had been the night with Lindsey in the parking lot of the Crab Shack since he'd had any physical release, and it wasn't a feeling Noah was used to. It wasn't like he couldn't go a day or two without sex; it was that he didn't want to. Ever since he was fifteen, there'd always been a girl or a woman to spend time with, but after his talk with Nick, he knew that had to change. But right now, he was having a hard time remembering why that was.

The restaurant near the harbor was busy, but he was able to find a small table in the corner. The waitress who came to take his order looked a little older than he was, but that wasn't a problem. His one and only relationship had been with an older woman, and even though it had ended, he still had great memories of the time. But this woman, with her messy blonde hair, short shorts, and halter top, could pass for twenty. She gave him a big smile, took his order for a Blue Moon on tap, and walked away, her hips swaying with the music coming over the loudspeaker.

37

On a different night he knew he would have plans with her before his dinner was served, but even though the thought of what was under that halter was working on his imagination, he was determined to stay true to his vow to Nick.

When the waitress brought his beer, he ordered the special to go. He could see the expression on her face fall when he didn't even ask her name, but she smiled and once again walked away. This time with a little less swagger.

17

Now

After a restless night's sleep, Noah was up with the sun, anxious to get to Louisiana and put together a team for the fishing tournament. He was sure that once *The Lark* had some paying customers looking to catch *the big one,* he'd get back his enthusiasm for being at sea. It bothered him a lot that he couldn't find the feelings he'd had since he was eighteen, but he chalked it up to a very unusual summer.

When he pulled into the marina in Venice, Louisiana, and saw all the people milling around on the dock, he felt a small thrill, the first since leaving AMI the day before. *I've been away too long,* he thought, *but I'll be fine once the tournament begins.*

The Lark was directed into a slip, and the port master came aboard with the requisite paperwork. After the two men talked about Noah's plans and the upcoming fishing tournament, the port master disembarked and left Noah on his own.

Home Run Charters and Lodge was a major part of the Louisiana fishing community, but the manager was a friend of his and always had more than enough customers to share. Not only were they a premiere charter outfit, but their lodge offered great accommodations for fishermen who came in from other areas, and that's what Noah was looking for.

"Hey old friend," Andy Croft said, coming around to shake Noah's hand. "It's about time you came back to visit."

The two men talked for a moment, catching up about why Noah had been absent from tournaments over the summer, and Andy shared the birth of his second child.

"Another girl?" Noah teased. "Are you going to make a fisherman out of this one?"

It was a big joke around the fishing community that Andy's first daughter wouldn't even touch a worm and thought the smell of fish was, "Scusting."

"That's kind of a sexist remark, don't you think, Greyson?" Andy joked. "Someday you'll have a kid, and if it's a girl, watch out."

Noah felt as if he'd had the wind knocked out of him. *Him a father?* Until Nick had told him about Lottie being pregnant, he'd only mildly thought about kids, but now? He was serious when he told Nick he wanted what he had, and Nick was only months away from being a dad.

"I think the first thing I need to do is find a woman who'll have me long enough to think about children, don't you?" he said, trying to get his breathing under control.

"If I remember right, the problem has never been having the woman stick around but getting you to make a commitment. Am I wrong?" Andy had a serious look on his face, and Noah was feeling very uncomfortable.

"I came here to fish, not talk about the ladies in my life, so help me out, okay?" Noah said, a little sharper than he intended.

Andy laughed. "I think I hit a nerve there, buddy, but sure I can help you put together a team."

Noah nodded, and let Andy continue. "I've got a group coming in tonight from Ohio, but the boat they were set to be on has some major engine problems. If you'd agree to take them, it would help us both out. I've been looking for a backup plan, and you may just be an answer to prayer."

"Sounds like it was meant to be," Noah answered. "What do you know about these guys? Are they good fisherman, or do I need to find a couple crew members?"

"They've been here before, and they can hold their own, but I'd still suggest you take on a couple of guys to crew for you. You want me to introduce you to some who haven't signed on with anyone yet?"

"I'd appreciate it," he told Andy. "The last thing I need is for someone to go overboard trying to reel in a bigger fish than he can handle."

Andy smiled in agreement and took Noah down to a group of ruddy looking men hoping to sign on with a boat.

"This here's Noah Greyson, a friend of mine from Florida. He's been here several times before, so you may have seen him around."

Andy waited for some recognition from the sailors and continued. "He needs a couple of good crew members for the fishing tournament that starts tomorrow; who's interested?"

A few of the hands went up, and one of the younger men asked. "Do you do this for a living?"

"I do," Noah replied, "but my brother was injured in July, and I needed to stay close to home. My dad owns the marina on Anna Maria Island, so *The Lark* and I both had a home for a few weeks." Noah pointed to his boat and was pleased when one of the men whistled.

"She's a beauty," he said, which seemed to be enough for the others, and soon they were following Noah down to *The Lark*.

After working out the business end of the fishing tournament and selecting two of the men to be his crew, Noah was feeling good. He told the guys what he would pay, even offering a bonus if they placed in the competition. He went over the rules he had for his charters, and told them he'd see them bright and early the next morning.

18

Now

It was only midafternoon, but Noah was starving. He'd had a banana earlier that morning, but that was all, and now his stomach was rumbling. He knew the area well, so he made sure everything was secured on the boat and started walking into town.

Venice, Louisiana was truly just the fishing village with an inhabitance of less than five hundred people. The town's nickname was, "The end of the world," because of its inaccessibility, but it had a diner/gas station/grocery store that served the best shrimp and grits Noah had ever tasted, and that's exactly where he was headed.

The ambiance in the Bait Bucket left a lot to be desired with its cement block walls and tin roof, but he was here for food, not refinement. Most of the booths were filled with locals sitting around and shootin' the bull, so Noah found a seat at the counter and waited to place his order. He'd been here enough times that he thought he knew everyone who worked there, so it was a pleasant surprise when he looked up from his menu to see a gorgeous Cajun beauty standing before him.

Without asking, she set an old coffee mug in front of him and filled it. Noah wasn't nearly the coffee drinker his brother was, but damned if he was going to start off on the wrong foot with the pretty girl who was pouring it. Instead he smiled and took a sip of the steaming hot brew.

Now he had a dilemma. Nick told him to stay out of bars, and technically this wasn't one, although they did sell beer by the can. But was there anything wrong with flirting a little? A man has to let off steam, he decided, so he put on his finest Greyson grin and gave her his best. And she shot him down.

This was totally new territory for Noah Greyson, and he kind of liked it. Girls had been throwing themselves at him ever since he'd reached puberty, so having one act indifferently was a challenge. He was up for it.

"So what can I get for you?" the girl asked politely. She had a nice southern drawl that he found sexy, even if she didn't mean for it to be.

"I'll have the shrimp and grits and an order of hush puppies," he answered, handing her back the menu. "Shirlene's still doing the cooking, right?"

"You know Shirlene?" the girl asked wide-eyed.

"Well sure I do," he grinned. "Everybody knows that Shirlene's the best cook in Venice."

The door from the kitchen swung open, and a tall, broad-shouldered woman of about sixty with skin the color of polished ebony walked out wearing an apron that read, *You can butter my biscuits anytime!*

"Noah Greyson, as I live and breathe!" she cackled. "I thought maybe the gators done ate you."

She came around the counter and gave Noah a hug and squeezed his butt. "You still got a nice ass for a sailor," she hooted and squeezed it again. "Tell me again why we never did any saliva swappin'?"

Noah backed away from her grabby hands and laughed. "Because you're too much woman for me, Shirlene, and you and I both know it."

"Have you met my granddaughter, Sissy?" the woman asked, a smile still on her face. "She belongs to my girl Ruby who ran off to Texas with that shady, white oil-man. He oiled something all right," she laughed.

Noah could see the embarrassment creeping up on the girl's face, and knew he needed to say something, but what? Finally he smiled her way and said, "I'd say she has your beautiful eyes and Ruby's smile. She looks like a yellow rose of Texas to me, and I'd say you should both be proud."

That made Sissy smile, and Shirlene added, "She's about to graduate from that fancy college in New Orleans. You know, Tulane."

Noah looked more closely at the young woman before him. Her hair was brown and rich, like pecans fresh from the tree, and her eyes, which did look like Shirlene's, were a warm chocolate brown. Her skin

43

was the color of coffee with cream, and he would never have guessed her to be Shirlene's granddaughter. But it was her mouth that was pulling him in. Full soft lips that were made for hot, slow kisses, and it was all he could do to keep the conversation moving.

"Tulane, huh?" he quizzed. "That is a fancy school; what are you studying?"

"I want to be a lawyer," Sissy said proudly. "I still have to graduate and go to law school of course, but I'm going to do it."

She was so emphatic that Noah didn't doubt her for a minute. He smiled and said, "Good for you, Sissy," but inside he was thinking, *but bad for me.* No way was he getting involved with a college girl with a bright future ahead of her. And especially not one whose grandmother he respected and truly liked. Nope, despite all of his instincts, Noah was leaving this girl alone.

After he all but licked the plate clean, Noah laid a twenty on the counter and started towards the door. He wasn't ten feet from making his escape when Shirlene called out.

"Hey, sailor. Sissy's done for the day, and I'd sure 'precciate it if you'd walk her home. All these men around town this week, I don't like her being out alone. That is of course, if you've got the time."

Noah ran his hands through his hair and looked back at Shirlene. How did you say no to that? She was right about there being a lot of men in town, and it probably wasn't safe for Sissy to be out alone, but he wasn't sure it was safe for her to be with him, either. But he nodded his acceptance and waited for Sissy to join him at the door.

"You didn't have to do this," she said, smiling at him with that kissable mouth. "Memaw forgets that I'm out by myself a lot when I'm at school. But I'm glad that you did."

They walked the few blocks to Shirlene's big two-story house, and Noah was impressed with how well taken care of it was. He didn't know much about Shirlene other than she was a widow, but this was a lot of house to maintain for anyone.

"This is a really nice house," Noah said honestly. "But seems like a lot of work for your grandma. Does she live here alone?"

Sissy shrugged her shoulders. "She rents out some rooms from time to time, and usually mowing the grass or planting some flowers is

44

part of the deal. Other than that, my Uncle Roscoe's boy Henry comes over and does the rest."

"Who does she rent rooms to?" Noah asked, wondering why anyone would be needing a room in Venice.

"Sailors," Sissy said, "but not when I'm here."

Noah walked Sissy up to the door and told her goodbye. She invited him in, but he told her honestly that he needed to go back to the boat and finish the arrangements for the next day's fishing tournament. On top of that, he knew being alone with her would only make him want things he knew shouldn't have.

19

Now

Noah woke up around three in the morning to the sound no fisherman wants to hear. Rain. He'd checked with the weather service before leaving home, and everything had looked good, so he was sure it was a pop-up shower and would end quickly. But by five, it was coming down heavier, and that was not a good sign.

He stepped out of the security of his berth and made a quick trip to the head. After brushing his teeth and splashing his face with cold water, he donned a pair of Frogg Toggs over jeans and a long-sleeved T-shirt and made his way topside. The main cabin was still dry, but the deck and the helm were taking a beating. Making sure everything was as secure as possible, he put his phone in the waterproof pouch of his pants and stepped onto the deck.

The rain was coming down in sheets, pelting him like a BB gun as he did his best not to be blown away. At six feet four, Noah Greyson was not a small man, but the wind and the rain were whipping at him like he was a young boy. Ahead he could see the lights of the lodge burning brightly like a beacon in the night, and as quickly as possible, he made his way inside.

"What the fuck!" he shouted to his friend Andy who was doing his best to shut the door. "Where in the hell did this come from?"

As a native of Venice, Andy Croft knew how quickly the weather could change along the Louisiana coastline, but this storm had him baffled as well. Shaking his head, he told his friend the truth. "It came out of nowhere. The weather service has it classified as a tropical depression, so I guess time will tell."

"So we sit on our butt and wait it out?" Noah asked.

"That's about all we can do," was Andy's reply. "Now get out of those wet clothes and come and meet the team I have lined up, and grab a cup of New Orleans style coffee. It'll warm you right up."

One sip of the coffee was all it took for Noah to know it was not for him. "What is this?" he asked making a face. "It's bitter as hell, and it's got milk in it."

Andy was laughing so hard he almost couldn't get the words out. "You mean in all your trips here you've never had our chicory coffee? Next I suppose you're going to tell me you've never had a Bourbon Street hooker either."

Noah's face got a little red, but he responded, "I don't kiss and tell, but I also don't drink piss, and that crap you gave me has to come close."

"Well it's all we've got this morning, so take it or leave it."

'I'm leaving it, thank you very much; now direct me to my team."

After taking off his wet gear, Noah followed Andy into a room of grumbling men. He didn't know if the bad moods were from the rain or the bad coffee, but he suspected a little bit of both.

"Noah, these are the men from Ohio I was telling you about," Andy said, pointing in the men's direction. "Gary Taylor, Sam Williams, and Michael Harris. Guys, this is my friend Noah Greyson. If the rain stops and we can have a tournament, he'd be a good captain for you to sign on with."

Noah stuck out his hand and acknowledged the men around him. Sam was the first to speak. "What are the chances there's really going to be a tournament?" he asked.

"I'll be honest with you," Andy said with a scowl on his face. "Slim to none, but you aren't going anywhere in this weather, so it's a good idea to have a game plan, just in case."

The men agreed and went back to their table to drink more of the awful coffee and wait for breakfast.

"So where can I get a cup of American coffee around here?" Noah teased Andy.

"Only place open will be the Bucket. Shirlene never closes unless a storm becomes an actual hurricane."

"Shirlene runs the Bait Bucket now?" Noah asked. "When did that happen?"

"How long's it been since you were here, buddy?" Andy laughed. "Shirlene not only runs the Bucket, she owns it. Rumor around town is she won it in a card game from old man Franklin, but I suspect he sold it to her. His kids up north have no interest in a Podunk operation like the Bait Bucket, but for Shirlene, it's been her whole life."

"Well I'll be damned," Noah said. Then he thought about Sissy and those soft pink lips waiting to be kissed and started putting back on his rain gear. "I'm going up for a real breakfast and to make sure Shirlene and Sissy are okay."

"You know Sissy, do you?" Andy winked. "The way I hear it, she doesn't take too kindly to our community."

"Maybe because they all want to drink that piss water you call coffee," Noah spat back, "but yeah, I know Sissy, and we get along just fine."

He was doing his best to open the door against the wind, but as he started out, he heard Andy chuckle and say, "I'll bet you do."

20

Now

Noah made it to The Bait Bucket by holding on to the buildings along the way. The storm hadn't gotten any worse, but the rain hadn't let up any either. It took all his strength to push the door open. Once he did, he was surprised at how busy the place was. Scanning the restaurant for Sissy, he could see that she was the only server, and she had her hands full.

"Hey sailor," she yelled out. "If you want coffee, the pot's on the counter, but if you want food, it's going to be a while. Marvis couldn't make it in today, but apparently the rest of the town could."

He heard the bell ding signifying an order was ready and saw the look of terror on Sissy's face. It was only seven o'clock in the morning, and already she was exhausted. Noah Greyson had never had a job other than working for Chester, but he'd been raised by a wonderful father and knew what his pop would expect him to do.

Peeling off his waterlogged rain gear, he hung them on an empty coat rack and picked the food off the counter as Shirlene was about to ring the bell a second time. When she saw Noah pick up the order, she gave him a big grin and said, "You know where you're going to take that?"

"I have no idea," he responded, but he knew how to find out. In his loudest voice Noah asked over the chatter, "Who ordered the western omelet and home fries?" A hand went up, and a new system was in place.

By the time the breakfast rush was clearing out, and he'd learned how to make Shirlene's special coffee brew without chicory, Noah was beat.

"How do you do this every day?" he asked Sissy as she was wiping down a table. "My feet and back are killing me."

The smile that spread across her face did a lot to take away any discomfort he was feeling.

"For a big strapping sailor, you sure do tire out quickly," she teased. "I would have thought reeling in those humongous fish would take more effort than waiting tables."

"That's a whole different kind of tired," he admitted, "but I definitely have renewed respect for waitresses now."

Shirlene stepped out of the kitchen with a platter covered with pancakes, bacon, and two eggs over easy. "You look like you need some nourishment," she grinned, "and besides, you earned it. If I recall, this is your favorite breakfast?"

Noah gave her cheek a quick peck and took the platter from her hands. Rich maple syrup and sweet cream butter were swimming over the stack of pancakes and slices of crisply fried bacon, with two fried eggs on the side, exactly the way he liked it.

"This looks like a feast fit for a king, Shirlene," he told her, shoveling in the first bite. "I'm not sure how you remembered about all this being my favorite, but it means a lot. Thank you."

Both Shirlene and Sissy watched him sandwich the eggs between the cakes, and then smear a slab in the sweetness of the syrup before putting it in his mouth. "So good," he moaned.

"It's downright repulsive, is what it is," Sissy told him, wrinkling up her nose. "How can you do that to my Memaw's cooking?"

"Now leave the boy alone, Sissy," Shirlene scolded. "I like to see a man enjoying my food. Anyway, we need to get this place cleaned up before the next rush comes in."

Noah was dragging his bacon through the runny egg yolk, hoping not to waste any of the golden goodness, but stopped to ask, "What can I do to help?"

"Did you bring all your gear in with you this morning?" Shirlene asked him.

"Just my phone, but everything else is locked up tight on *The Lark*."

"Then what you can do for me is clean your plate and then run down to the dock for the rest of your things. No way you're sleeping on that boat for the next couple days."

"I've been in storms lots of times, Shirlene. *The Lark* and I'll be fine."

The look she gave him was the same one Pop used when he was in trouble as a kid, but it had been a lot of years since he'd seen it.

"You listen to me, Noah Greyson," she demanded. "I've lived in these parts a long time, and this isn't a storm you want to mess with. Now, go get your things while I finish up some gumbo and corn chowder. If we lose power, folks are gonna need something to eat, and I've got the only generator in town."

Noah scrubbed his face with his hands, trying to think of what to say. "The thing is, Shirlene, I'm sure the lodge is full up, but I appreciate your concern, I really do."

"It makes no never mind because you're not sleeping at the lodge, you're coming to my house. I'll need to stay here and keep an eye on the Bucket, and you're going to watch over Sissy and my home. You got any questions?"

Noah gulped and said, "No ma'am."

21
Now

This walk back to the harbor was even more difficult than the one coming in that morning, and for the first time, Noah was concerned. He was being truthful when he told Shirlene he'd been out in storms before, but there was something about this one that felt different. The wind and the rain were hitting him in the head like shards of glass as he crept along the now-deserted streets. After his morning helping at the restaurant, every inch of his body felt achy and cold.

The light was on at the lodge, and Noah decided to stop there on his way back to the Bait Bucket. He wanted Andy to know where he'd be, and he needed Pop to know that he was okay.

The boats were swaying as the wind rushed around them, and he felt a knot in his stomach thinking about the damage *The Lark* might sustain. Pushing through his fatigue, he climbed aboard and took a quick inventory. So far the only problem was the water covering the deck, but he knew his girl was made to withstand more than rain. The cabin and berth were still dry, so Noah grabbed his duffle bag of clothes and threw in his phone charger, flashlight, emergency radio, book, and the cash he'd brought with him. He thought twice about taking the gun that he kept locked in a special compartment under his bed, but finally decided it wasn't safe to leave it on the boat, locked up or not. Taking one last look around, he pulled the hood of his Frogg Togg jacket tightly around his face and braced himself for another onslaught of pounding rain.

Andy must have seen him hobbling up the steps because he had the door open before Noah even got there. "Holy crap, Greyson," he said. "Don't you know enough to come in out of the rain?"

Noah was in no mood to banter. "I'm tired and waterlogged so please, spare me, okay? I came to tell you I'll be staying up at Shirlene's, at least overnight if you need me. Now hand over your phone."

"Why do you want my phone?" Andy asked, handing his phone to Noah.

"I'm going to put in my number, so you have a way to reach me. Before I leave, I need to call my dad and give him your number, so he has at least two ways to contact me. You good with that?"

Andy nodded and took back his phone. "Maybe you should give me your dad's number as well, in case I need to call him."

"I already did. Now, can I go into your office so I can call Pop without having all the chatter in the background?"

Andy walked him through the hallway and into an office tastefully decorated to look like the captain's quarters on a yacht. "Obviously you charge too much," Noah said sarcastically. "Good thing I'll be staying with Shirlene for free."

"Maybe no money will change hands, but I'm not sure Shirlene gives anything for free," Andy joked. "But then again, you'll be alone with that sweet little granddaughter of hers and—"

"That's enough," Noah said with so much force that even he was taken back. "Sissy's a good kid, and I won't have you talking like that about her. Don't forget, your girls are going to be her age someday."

Andy looked as if he'd been slapped in the face as he raised his hands in surrender. "You better call your dad," he said and walked out of the office.

After talking with Pop, Noah felt more at ease, and he went looking for Andy. He found him alone in the kitchen, nursing a beer and looking like a lost puppy.

"Hey, Andy," Noah said giving his friend a pat on the back. "I'm sorry for getting a little fired-up before. I had no right bringing up your kids."

Andy nodded and took a swig of the beer. "The thing is, you were right. My girls are going to grow up and the last thing I want is some guy looking at them as just a piece of tail. You've given me a lot to think about, and I'm afraid this storm is going to give me the time I need to do it."

53

He reached his arm out in Noah's direction, and the two men shook hands like the old friends that they were. As Noah walked away, he was hit with an uncomfortable thought. Most of his life he'd been using women because he couldn't have the one woman that he wanted. Now he was doing his best to change his image and find a woman to share his life with, and he had no clue where to begin. Was that irony or not?

22

Then

Noah entered the locker room after gym class and heard the raucous laughing. Two guys were having a tug-of-war match with a wet towel while they laughed and taunted each other.

"You wouldn't stand a chance in hell of getting close to them," one of the guys laughed.

"I'd come closer than you would," the other shouted back.

The towel they were pulling on snapped lose and ended up in Noah's face.

"What the heck?" he asked, throwing the towel on the floor.

"Riley and I were just talking about Lottie's rack, and how we'd like to be the first guy to man-handle it," Mike Potter chuckled. "But I think she's got those things under lock and key." Potter, nicknamed Pothead, grabbed the towel off the floor just as Noah grabbed him.

"What the hell, Greyson," he demanded, trying to pull free. "Don't tell me you've already picked the lock? I thought you liked the ladies over at Bradenton?"

Noah had quite a reputation as a player, but only because the girl he wanted was his brother's best friend. But that didn't mean he was going to stand there and let these jerks talk about her the way they were.

He didn't remember throwing the first punch, but the next thing he knew he was rolling on the floor and wrestling with Pothead, the other guys cheering them on. That is, until Coach Donavan walked in.

The coach had to blow his whistle twice and physically yank the boys apart to get them to stop fighting. "Break it up I said!"

Finally, Noah saw and heard Coach Donavan and pulled away from Pothead but not before giving him one more shove.

"That's enough," Coach told the boys and then taking them each by an arm pulled them into his office.

"The rest of you get dressed and get out of here," he growled to the remainder of the class. "The show's over."

Noah ended up being suspended from school, but it had been worth it. No one was going to talk about Lottie like that when he was around.

23
Now

Noah fought his way back to the Bait Bucket, the wind pushing him around like he was a kite. He was as wet and tired as he could ever remember and wanted nothing more than a hot shower and a soft bed, but when he finally pushed open the door to the restaurant, he was amazed to see that it was once again filled with people.

Sissy was carrying a tray loaded with big bowls of steaming soup and plates covered with thick slices of bread and butter but was able to give him a half smile when she walked by. He shook his head and took off his waterlogged rain gear, knowing that he was in for another round of customer service.

"Shirlene," he hollered through the kitchen's pick-up window, "where are all these people coming from? It's a damn monsoon out there."

"Don't you be swearing in my restaurant, Noah Greyson," she scolded. "This here's a fine establishment, and I'll thank you to remember that."

Her arms were crossed across her chest in defiance, and Noah backed down like a shamed puppy. "I'm sorry, Shirlene," he said contritely. "It's just that these people need to go home and get ready in case this thing turns into a hurricane. I'm telling you, the Bucket needs to close, and you need to let me help you and Sissy get home now."

Shirlene shook her head. "The people you're looking at don't really have homes," she told him. "'Cept that shantytown over yonder. They'll be staying here with me until the storm passes, but you and Sissy can be on your way as soon as everyone gets fed."

Shantytown? He had no idea. Noah ran his hands through his damp, dirty blond hair and smiled at her. "You're good people,

Shirlene, you know that? Now you keep ladling out that soup, and I'll help Sissy make sure everyone gets their fill."

By the time the last person was dipping their bread in the steamy rich gumbo, Noah was dead on his feet. He'd heard the ping of his phone a couple of times signaling messages, but when your hands are full of heavy trays of food or stacked high with dirty dishes, you don't stop to answer a text. He knew if it was important, the person would call, so he left the messages to look at later.

Finally, the last person had been fed, and most of the dishes had been rinsed and loaded into the big commercial dishwasher in Shirlene's kitchen. Noah was contemplating whether or not he could even walk the short way to Shirlene's house when he looked up and saw two sheriff's deputies, each with their arms laden with supplies, enter the restaurant.

"Here you go, Shirlene," said one of the deputies. "We rounded up every available blanket in town; will it be enough?"

"Bless your heart, Will Badgett," she said. "You're an angel in disguise. Now, sit yourself down, and let me fix you a bowl of my special recipe chowder. I'd offer you gumbo, but I'm fresh out."

"I appreciate the offer, but we need to get back out on the streets," he told her. "No telling when we're all going to be called in."

"Do you have time to do me one more favor?" Shirlene asked.

"You know I'd do most anything for you, Shirlene," the young deputy smiled. "It was you made my Suzanna give me a chance a few years back, and now look at us, married almost a year."

"I didn't do nothing but point that girl in the right direction," Shirlene beamed, "but I'm sure glad it all worked out."

"So what is it I can do for you?" he asked.

"I need my granddaughter to get home and tend to my babies. If you'd give her and my friend Captain Greyson a ride to my house, I'd sure be obliged. It ain't fit for them to be walking."

Noah heard the word babies and his ears perked up. *What kind of babies could Shirlene have that she'd left home alone all day?*

Sissy could see the gears turning in his head and laughed. "Miss Scarlet is Memaw's calico, and Rhett Butler is her big old hound dog. She treats them like royalty," she laughed.

"Miss Scarlet and Rhett Butler?" he quizzed.

"She loves *Gone With the Wind,*" said Sissy. "My real name is Sierra, but Memaw said that sounded too much like the desert, so she's called me Sissy ever since I can remember. I meant what I said, she loves that book."

Noah shook his head but couldn't keep from laughing. Shirlene was one surprise after another.

"You two go on now and get out of here while you've got a ride." Shirlene told them, "Deputy Will's a busy man."

"I really think we should stay here with you," Noah tried to reason.

"Did you not hear me say my babies need taken care of?" she grumbled. "Besides, you look like you're about dead on your feet, and I've got a big feather bed over home with your name on it."

"I'm not any more tired than you and Sissy," Noah protested, although the words *feather bed* were going round and round in his head. "I don't like leaving you alone here."

Shirlene looked a little misty eyed when she responded. "You've been more help today than most any man has been in my life but trust me; I'll be okay. These fine deputies from the sheriff's department will be around to check on things and grab fresh coffee, so don't you worry 'bout us at all. You make sure my Sissy arrives home safely, and you take care of her; you hear?"

Shirlene handed Noah two large containers filled with chowder and sandwiches and did her best to hurry him out the door. He put on his wet rain gear while Sissy buttoned up her coat and hugged her grandmother goodbye.

They were only going a couple of blocks, but as she walked out the door, Sissy called out, "I'll let you know when we get there, Memaw. I love you."

"I love you, too, baby girl," Shirlene called back. "I love you, too."

24

Now

The ride to Shirlene's house from the Bait Bucket shouldn't have taken more than five minutes, but the streets were starting to flood, and Deputy Badgett was being cautious. When they finally pulled up, Noah wrestled against the wind to get the back door of the cruiser opened, and Sissy slid over and stepped out. He handed her his duffle bag and motioned for her to get inside while he reached for the containers of food Shirlene sent with them.

"You really will check on things at the Bucket, won't you?' he asked the deputy.

"Yes sir, I really will," he replied. "I'm not sure I've seen you around these parts before, but you seem to really care about Shirlene. If you or Sissy needs anything, call the station and ask for Will."

Noah was in a shoving match with the storm, and the storm was winning, but he stopped a minute to think about the deputy's words. He did care about Shirlene, and the last thing he wanted to do was let her down.

Before he could even make it to the back door, a big brown hound dog came barreling out of nowhere, jumping up to lick Noah's face and then sticking his head in to sniff his crotch.

"Rhett Butler you stop that this instant!" Sissy hollered, but between the noise of the wind howling and the smell of food from the containers Noah was trying to hold on to, the old dog had no intention of backing down. Instead he jumped up again, and this time Noah lost his footing in the mud and went down hard.

"Fuck!" he yelled, doing his best to keep the food out of the dog's reach. Sissy rushed out the door to his rescue, but it was a lost cause. Pretty quickly they were both soaking wet, covered with mud, and laughing out loud. Not understanding what was going on, Rhett Butler sat down beside them and began to howl.

Somehow the sandwiches and chowder were saved, but Noah felt as if he had mud in every crevice of his body. His boots were covered; there was even mud inside his socks and there was no way he was tracking that kind of mess in Shirlene's house. Sissy was no better off and even had leaves and little twigs sticking out of her hair. They stood on the old back porch, soaking wet, shivering, and contemplating what to do, while Miss Scarlet sat on her perch cleaning her paws. It was obvious she thought they were both nuts.

Sissy saw an old towel lying by the door and was certain it belonged to Rhett Butler. But they were desperate, and she came up with a plan.

"How about if I leave my clothes here, wrap up in that towel and run upstairs and get one for you? Then we can take turns getting a shower and put this day behind us." Noah was so tired that even the thought of a shower sounded like too much effort, but as Sissy told him her plan, and he thought about her naked body with nothing but a towel wrapped around it, he started to come to life.

"The gentlemanly thing would be for me to offer to go first, but since I don't know where anything is, I accept your offer." It had been too long since he'd had a warm nubile body underneath him, and the thought of it had him hard. Trying to move so she wouldn't notice the bulge in his jeans he added, "Go on, I promise not to look."

Sissy's eyes got big and she blushed, but what choice did she have? She grabbed the towel and as quickly as possible, removed her soaking wet uniform and bra. When she reached her panties, she thought twice about taking them off, but they, too, were covered in thick, dark mud. With one swoop they were off and added to the pile of clothing to probably be thrown away.

Noah heard her scampering into the house and opened one eye just a little. He said he wouldn't look but that was different than a peek wasn't it? Unfortunately, his plan failed, because once he caught site of her luscious backside, he knew he was in deep shit.

Sissy returned wrapped in a bath sheet and told him it was his turn. Noah had never been bashful around women, but this was different.

61

"Aren't you going to go shower?" he asked before even slipping off his T-shirt.

"Nope," she said with a twinkle in her eye.

"Then at least you need to promise not to look, like I did."

"You see that big old pot hanging over the stove?" Sissy asked him.

"Yeah, what about it?" Noah asked cautiously.

"Well," she went on, biting on her bottom lip just enough to make him crazy, "I could see your reflection as I took off, and you were definitely looking, Noah Greyson, right after you promised that you wouldn't."

"I wasn't looking," he tried to reason with her, "it was just a peek. One tiny peek."

"Fair enough," Sissy said with a saucy smile. "That's all I'm asking for, too. Just one peek."

25

Now

Shirlene had been right about the feather bed, it was a little bit of heaven on earth. Especially for a man who had been awake since three o'clock, fought the wind and the rain multiple times, served and bussed tables in a restaurant, and fought every instinct he had not to throw a hot little temptress over his shoulder and fuck her senseless.

But he hadn't, even though he'd thought about it all night, and now here it was morning, and the storm seemed to have no end in sight. Noah grabbed his Dopp kit and headed to the bathroom to shave and brush his teeth. The shower the night before had at least taken the sweat and the grime off of his body, but he'd been so tired that he hadn't done anything else. Now, he needed to get rid of what the commercials called *morning breath.*

The bathroom door was open halfway, and without even thinking, Noah walked in. There he found Sissy in a short, almost see-through nighty of pale pink, and the ache he'd been feeling in his groin started spreading to his heart.

She was perfect in all the ways a woman should be; smart, gorgeous, caring, and fun to be around, but she was way too young for him, *wasn't she?* Backing out of the bathroom with a soft apology, Noah knew that he needed to talk with Nick and talk with him now.

He stepped back into the bedroom with the amazing feather bed and found his phone. But when he opened it to call his brother, the first thing he saw was three messages from Stella.

> *Hi Noah! I heard about the storm in Louisiana and just wanted to check on you. Let me know that you're okay.*

Hey, I'm starting to worry. I know you can take care of yourself, but the news is talking about nothing but the storm and I know you were headed that way. Please just let me know everything is okay.

I know we're only buds, Noah Greyson, but you're scaring me. If I don't hear back from you this morning, I'm calling Nick.

The last message had just arrived while he was in the bathroom ogling Sissy, so Noah quickly sent Stella a response, knowing the last thing he wanted was for her to reach out to his brother.

Sorry I worried you, Stella, but I'm fine. I'm in Louisiana, pretty much in the middle of the storm, but I found a place to stay in an older woman's house, so I'm off the water. I hope your modeling gig is going well, talk soon.

A place to stay in an older woman's house. Why did he say that? Stella wouldn't care where he was staying, why didn't he just tell her? Possibly because it was a quick text, but probably because he wanted her to think of him as a standup guy and not a womanizer. Why that mattered he didn't know. He was putting his phone away when Sissy knocked on the door.

"You talking to your girlfriend?" she asked after seeing him with his phone.

"No, no girlfriend," he told her. "Well it was a girl, but truly just a friend. She wanted to make sure I was safe."

Sissy smiled and nodded. "You interested in some breakfast?" she asked. "I'm not anywhere as good a cook as my Memaw, but I can scramble an egg."

"Or how about," Noah told her as he got up off the bed, "I cook for you. I make pretty mean French toast, if I do say so myself."

"You can cook?" Sissy asked in amazement. "My mom has never been around much, so I learned bits and pieces from my Memaw."

64

"My mom wasn't around much either," he replied. "But my Pop taught us all how to cook when we were growing up. He's pretty amazing."

"Who's us?" she asked, and his call to Nick was all but forgotten.

26

Then

Sunday mornings Pop always fixed a big breakfast and was usually happy to comply with his kid's requests. But for some reason this Sunday he had a different plan.

"Can we have eggs in a basket for breakfast?" Maya asked.

"I was hoping for sausage gravy and biscuits," Nick said.

"And I want French toast," Noah chimed in. "Maybe we should go out to eat."

"Or maybe," Pop chuckled, "it's time you all learned to cook so you can fix your own breakfasts."

"Way to go, jerks," complained fifteen-year-old Maya. "Now I have to learn a domestic skill."

"Now, Maya," Pop had lightly scolded. "Someday you'll be glad that you know how to cook, and in the meantime, I won't have to listen to you three grumble every Sunday morning.

The three Greyson kids moaned at first, but it wasn't long until they were laughing and enjoying their cooking lesson. Nick danced around the kitchen, holding a wooden spoon like a microphone, as Maya and Noah sang and clapped their hands. The kitchen was a mess, but even Pop seemed to be relishing the moment.

When they sat down to eat, Maya ended up having French toast; Nick had eggs in a basket, and Noah had the sausage gravy and biscuits. At that moment, they probably couldn't have told you why, but years later, after Nick had been shot and was lying in a coma, Noah knew. There was a bond between them that nothing could break. They'd been *The Three Musketeers,* but now they were a family. They were the Greysons. And they stood united.

27

Now

After a breakfast of French toast and sausage links, Noah and Sissy washed and dried the dishes and tidied up the old-fashioned kitchen. The rain was still coming down hard, and even Rhett Butler was content to stay inside.

While Sissy was watching the weather on TV, Noah slipped away to shave and brush his teeth. The two-day growth on his face was more than a five o'clock shadow, and he decided he kind of liked it. Made him look more like a fisherman. Putting the razor away, he brushed his teeth and decided this might be a good time to call Nick. *But to say what?*

"Hey, little brother," Nick answered. "Pop says you're in the middle of chaos but riding the storm out at some boarding house? How are you holding up?"

"Where do I begin?" Noah sighed. "This rain is like nothing I've ever experienced, and Sissy just said the storm has been upgraded from a tropical depression to a tropical storm."

"Sissy, huh?" Nick asked. "Only you could find a hook-up in the middle of a storm. I thought you were going to grow up and quit bed hopping. Isn't that what you told me the other day?"

"I'm not bed hopping, and Sissy isn't a hook-up," Noah growled, "She lives here. I haven't been with a woman since that night with Lindsey, but how did you do it, Nick? You must have had the bluest balls in Florida."

"What are you talking about, Noah?" Nick laughed.

"You know, you told me to stay out of bars, and I have, but I'm not like you, Nick. I can't go without sex."

"What makes you think I did?" Nick chuckled. "I may not have been the ladies' man you are, but I did okay. You said you wanted what I have, so I told you to stay out of the bars. That doesn't mean you can't take a woman to bed; it means you need to get to know her first. Do you understand what I'm saying?"

Shifting gears, Noah asked another question. "How young is too young do you think?"

"Speaking as a former law enforcement official, I'll tell you that you don't want to even look at a girl under eighteen. That's a sure way to end up as a registered sex offender, even if the girl agrees. Plus, I don't think you'd do well in prison. Speaking as your brother and someone who knows you pretty well, I'd say at least twenty-one. You're going to want a woman you can buy a drink." Nick stopped to let his words sink in and then continued. "Why are you asking me this?"

Noah wasn't ready to tell him about the thoughts he was having about Sissy, so he did his best to act nonchalant. "Just want to make sure I know the ground rules is all."

"Be careful, Noah, that's all I can say. Be selective in the women you sleep with and always use protection."

"This coming from the man who got his wife pregnant before she was even his girlfriend?" Noah smirked.

"Okay, wise-ass," Nick spat back. "You've made your point; is there anything else I can do for you?"

Noah quickly became serious. "Thanks Nick. I am trying to make better choices, and I appreciate your advice, really. So, how's married life treating you?" he asked.

"Charlotte's learning to cook," Nick told him. "And guess who's giving the lessons?"

"Pop?" Noah asked even though he was sure of the answer. "I was thinking this morning about the Sunday he taught us how to make our own breakfasts. Those were some great times, weren't they?"

"They were the best, Noah, and it's what I want for my family and for you." Nick had definitely put back on his big brother hat, so Noah asked one more question.

"Lottie's the only girl I've ever loved," he said cautiously, "do you think I'll ever be able to feel that way about someone else?"

"That's going to be up to you," Nick answered. "You kept those feelings hidden for years, but now that you've admitted them you need to let them go. There's a perfect woman out there just waiting for you; but you need to go find her."

When they hung up, Noah wasn't sure if he had the answer to his dilemma, but he did feel better. Somehow just talking to Nick or Pop made everything look brighter, and on a dark, rainy day, brighter is exactly what he needed.

He and Sissy kept the TV on so they could stay abreast of the storm activity, and she called Shirlene to check on things at the Bait Bucket. Satisfied that her Memaw was okay, Sissy asked Noah if he wanted to play Scrabble.

"Seriously?" he questioned. "I haven't played a board game with anyone but my nieces in years, but I used to be pretty good. But sure, let's play."

Sissy got the game down from the hall closet, and while she set it up, she asked Noah to tell her about his family. They played for a good two hours before Sissy started to yawn.

"I think I need a nap," she admitted, pushing away from the table.

"You're only saying that because I came up with schnozz and got thirty points." Noah teased her. "Don't be a sore loser."

"I'll expect a rematch later," she laughed. "No pretty boy from a swanky island is going to beat me!"

"You think I'm pretty?" Noah asked her with a twinkle in his eye.

"I'm taking a nap," Sissy snapped. "Don't bother me for at least an hour!"

28

Now

Sissy settled on the couch and was asleep in minutes. Noah watched her chest rise and fall and decided it was making him want things that he knew he shouldn't, so he headed to the room where he had slept the night before. He pulled the book out of his duffle bag and settled in the big comfortable feather bed. He hadn't slept well the night before, and the rain hitting the tin roof and the dark sky coming through the windows lulled him right to sleep.

"Noah," he heard, trying to come out of his sleep induced fog. "I'm scared; can I be in here with you?"

The voice was so faint that at first that he thought it was coming from the TV in the living room, but when he opened his eyes, he saw Sissy climbing in the bed beside him.

"Uh, Sissy," he said, wiping his eyes. "What are you doing?"

"I had a bad dream, and when I woke up it was dark, and I was alone. Can I stay in here with you?" she pleaded.

"Maybe it would be better if I got up and we went back to the living room," Noah said.

"I don't want to go back in there," Sissy said as she reached up and stroked his face. "I want to stay right where we are."

Her hair smelled like fresh apples Noah noticed, and her lips, those damn kissable lips, were slightly parted and almost begging him to have a taste. His voice husky with desire he tried once more to reason with her.

"You know what you're saying, Sissy?" he asked her. "Because I don't think I can keep my hands off of you if we don't get out of this bed right now."

Sissy took his hand and placed it on her full, firm breast. "Then don't."

The first kiss was better than he ever could have imagined. She moaned as he explored every inch of her luscious mouth, and when she nipped at his bottom lip, he almost came unglued. Slipping his hand under her shirt and feeling the smooth skin of her back, Noah hesitated. But when Sissy started kissing down his neck and encouraging him with her soft expressions, he continued. Finding the hooks on her bra, he unclasped it, his fingers shaking like a schoolboy, but he didn't want to do anything to ruin this moment.

Her breasts were warm and soft and felt like satin against his rough hands. Her nipples were taut and begging to be teased, and when he did, Sissy cried out in pleasure. Noah was moving slowly, not wanted to scare her, but it wasn't fast enough. In one swift motion, she threw off her shirt and bra and tossed them on the bed.

Noah looked into her chocolate brown eyes and lifted his mouth to the offering before him. He licked and sucked and gently pulled on her swollen flesh with his teeth, feeling her let go as he did. *Damn!* He'd never know a woman to have an orgasm just from having her breasts worshipped, but it was a heady feeling, knowing that he'd been the cause of it.

"Are you okay?" he asked, not sure whether he should go on or not.

"I'm better than okay," Sissy smiled. "Why are you stopping?"

Noah gave her a cocky grin and moved his fingers to the snap on her jeans. "I'm not done," he teased her. "Only giving you a chance to get ready for the main event. And by the way, how old are you?"

"Not sure why you're asking," Sissy said, wiggling her ample bottom out of her jeans. "But I'm twenty-two."

"I might want to take you out for a drink sometime," Noah said, remembering Nick's suggestion. "I need to know that you're legal."

"Oh, I'm legal alright," she said, working feverishly to remove Noah's shirt. "But the only place around here to get booze is a six pack at Memaw's store. You could always come to New Orleans; we could have lots of fun there. Now, quit talking and show me that main event."

"I might take you up on that," Noah replied, and then she sealed his mouth with hers and all talking came to a halt.

71

Two hours later they were lying side by side, holding hands, and trying to catch their breath. Sissy recovered first and leaned over Noah's chest leaving soft small kisses down his torso. When she got to his happy trail, where the hair became curly and coarse, Noah shifted his large body to deter her access.

"Slow down there, counselor," he told her. "I'm going to need to rest up before I'm up for round three."

Sissy gave him a sly smile but lay back down. "Technically, it would be round four for you," she said, pointing to the three condom wrappers on the floor. "But I understand at your advanced age it takes time to recover."

"My advanced age!" he said, reaching over to tickle her tummy. "How old do you think I am?"

"I don't know, and I don't care," she laughed, "But I wish you could have seen the look on your face."

Noah cupped her face in his hand and gave her a long, slow kiss. "Give me thirty minutes and I'm all yours," he told her gently, and wrapping her in his arms, he fell asleep.

29
Now

When Noah woke up, Sissy was gone but the place where she'd been lying was still warm. He pulled the pillow that had cradled her head to his chest and smiled as he again picked up the scent of apples. He could hear noises coming from the kitchen as he carefully pulled on his jeans. They hadn't made it to round four yet, but he could feel the effects of their afternoon delight when the rough denim scrapped against his skin.

It was hard to keep the smile off his face when he walked into the kitchen and saw Sissy standing at the stove, wearing a pair of baggy sweatpants and a T-shirt that hung down to her knees. If he hadn't seen firsthand what a delicious body was hiding under the sloppy outfit, he'd have never believed it himself. But he had, and now the thought of tasting her again and making her scream out his name had him ready for that elusive next round.

Sissy turned around as Noah was creeping up on her. "Don't think I can't hear you, Noah Greyson," she teased. "Miss Scarlet and I both have exemplary hearing." She turned around and melted against his body while Miss Scarlet sat on her perch and mewed.

"Memaw called," Sissy said, pulling back so she could talk. "Evidently while we were napping, the power flickered off and on in town, and she suggested we have an early dinner, in case it goes out for good. I'm warming up the chowder and getting ready to slice some tomatoes and onions to put on the sandwiches. Is that enough for you?"

It was all he could do not to take her right there in the kitchen, but Noah nodded. "Maybe no onion though," he said with a smile, and Sissy got his drift.

"You didn't say anything to Shirlene about, well you know, earlier, did you?" Noah asked. The last thing he wanted was to get his ass kicked by someone's grandmother.

Sissy was having a hard time not laughing. "You mean did I tell her that the big ole sea captain that she asked to protect me took me to bed and had his way with me? And that he knows how to do lots of wicked things with that pretty mouth of his?"

Noah could feel his face heating up. "Very funny," he grumbled. "I guess I knew you didn't say anything, but I really do like your grandmother, and I don't want to let her down."

Sissy got on her tiptoes and kissed his nose. "I really like her, too," she told him. "But knowing my Memaw, she'd be happy to know what went on here today. But don't worry, I have no plans to tell her."

When the soup was hot, they put slices of fresh tomatoes on the sandwiches that Shirlene had sent home with them the day before and sat down at the kitchen table to eat. Sissy had already set the little table and put out a pitcher of cold, sweet tea, and as Noah looked around, he realized how much he was enjoying the domesticity before him. And that made his heart race.

After dinner they washed and dried the dishes, sharing the plans they each had for the future as they worked. Sissy had a semester left in her undergraduate degree, and then she was going to use the second half of the year to prepare for her LSATs. Being a lawyer had been her dream since her Memaw had taken her to see *Legally Blonde* at the old drive-in theater when she was five.

"I even thought about dying my hair blonde before I left for Tulane," she told him honestly. "But Memaw told me about some guy named Polonius, and being true to myself, so I thought better of it. How about you, sailor, what are you going to do with the rest of your life?"

At that very moment Noah wanted to say, *stay right here with you,* but he knew that was the sex and the situation talking. What did he want to do with the rest of his life? He wasn't truly sure, so he told her about his dreams of taking *The Lark* on an ocean voyage, but even as he said them, he realized they weren't true anymore.

The dishes done and the kitchen clean, Noah forced Rhett Butler out the back door and into the pouring rain. The old dog did his business quickly and howled his displeasure at Noah when he let him in. Sissy turned off the light and made sure that both of their cell phones were plugged in before checking on the weather forecast.

"It says the rain's letting up," she told Noah, "but it still looks awfully spooky out. Maybe we should go to bed now, and when we wake up tomorrow, the storm will be over." The look she was giving him was all it took for him to understand her meaning.

Noah took her hand and said, "This time we're going to do things right." Leading Sissy gently towards the bathroom, he started water running in the old claw foot tub and pulled the beautiful young woman into his arms. After a deep passionate kiss, he threw some of the orange blossom bath salts that were sitting on the counter into the water and began undressing her.

Noah was on his knees by the time he got to her panties and could feel Sissy trembling beneath his touch. Almost tortuously slow, he slipped the little piece of lace down past her thighs, staring into her eyes the whole time. When she lifted her foot to allow the panties to be removed, Noah started placing kisses up her thigh.

"Noah," she said, trying to catch her breath, but he touched her lips with his finger and shook his head.

"I'm going to remind you of the wicked things I can do with my mouth," he whispered, as he explored her most intimate parts with his tongue. When she cried out, he held onto her legs to keep her from falling and helped her into the fragrant steaming water.

30
Now

Why is it so quiet? was his first thought of the day. *Where is the patter of rain falling on the roof and the sound of wind rustling through the trees?* Sissy was snuggled beside him, with Miss Scarlet nestled in the crook of her legs, and as gingerly as possible, Noah slipped out of bed.

He peeked out the window and saw the beginning of a morning sky. Part of him wanted to jump for joy, and part of him wanted to climb back in bed and put his arms around the beauty who had slept beside him. Noah knew that the last two days had been magical, but now that the storm had ended, his time with Sissy would change. He just wasn't sure yet how.

"Noah," she said, stretching and letting out a big yawn. "Come back to bed."

"Don't you hear that, Sissy?" he asked. "That's the sound of a storm that's ended."

She jumped out of bed and joined him at the window. "I've got to go call Memaw," she exclaimed, clapping her hands. "I'll bet she needs help at the Bucket." Sissy ran in to get her phone, and Noah headed for the shower. He was anxious to get to the dock and see how *The Lark* had fared, and he knew Sissy was right. Shirlene was going to be needing her granddaughter's help.

The shower felt good, and Noah spent an extra minute letting the hot water run down over his body. He'd felt the ache in his groin before from needing a woman, but this was the first time he'd felt an ache from having too much woman. He smiled as he thought of Sissy and the amazing night they'd spent together. He didn't know what the future might hold for them, but he was sure excited about finding out.

Dried, dressed, and packed, Noah went into the kitchen to see if he could help Sissy with breakfast. He was picturing her standing at the stove again and thought once more about how it had felt to make love to her. As sore as he was, he wouldn't turn her down if she gave him that look, but when he reached the kitchen, he found Sissy sitting at the kitchen table, her cell phone in her hand.

"What's wrong?" he asked, dropping his duffle bag to wrap his arms around her. "Is it Shirlene, or a problem at the Bucket?"

Sissy shook her head, and when she looked up at him, Noah could see the tears in her eyes and could feel the cannon ball sinking in his stomach.

"Noah," she started, and he knew then he wasn't going to like what she had to say.

"My boyfriend called."

"Your boyfriend" Noah demanded, feeling as if a knife was being shoved in his back.

"He was my boyfriend, but…"

Noah hung his head and ran his hands through his hair. "I don't know what to say. You have a special guy in your life and yet we…, you let me…what the hell, Sissy?"

He was angry now, but when the tears in her eyes became sobs, Noah felt like shit. He hadn't meant to lash out at her, but just when he let himself see her as more than a hot body between the sheets, this happened. Was it the Universe's way of paying him back for his escapades with girls like Lindsey? He scrubbed his face with his hand and put his arms around the crying woman.

"I'm sorry, Sissy," he said as he stroked her hair. "I didn't mean to yell, but you caught me off guard. I wouldn't hurt you for the world, but I never would have let things get out of hand if I have known there was another man in the picture."

He did his best to calm her down, and when she did, Noah said, "I think we have some things to talk about."

"I shouldn't have said my boyfriend," Sissy said, still sniffling, "We broke up when I came home for summer break."

"That's something," Noah replied. "But if you broke up why did he call?"

"Because he wants me back," she answered softly.

Noah nodded and said to her, "Maybe you should start at the beginning so that I can decide whether or not to feel like a jerk."

"Malcom...that's his name, comes from a long line of distinguished attorneys and judges in New Orleans, and that's how we met. He's already in law school and has a place in his family's firm when he graduates."

"Go on," was all he said.

"We started dating two years ago, but he never would introduce me to his family. A few weeks before the end of the semester we had a big fight when I said I wanted to meet his family. He'd already met Memaw and my mama, so it seemed only right, don't you think?" The look on her face was breaking his heart, but Noah didn't say a word.

"Here's the thing," she finally said with a sigh, "he finally found the nerve to tell me that his family won't like me because, well you know, because of my heritage."

Noah was seeing red! How dare some snot nosed rich boy turn away from Sissy because of her Afro-American lineage? If that Malcom character was there right now, Noah wasn't sure he could be held responsible for his actions. "Oh, Sissy," he said, pulling her towards him. "You're everything a man could ever want, and if Malcom won't see past the color of your mother's skin then he isn't worthy of you, can't you see that?"

"Wait," she told him. "You've got it wrong. It isn't my mother's dark skin his family doesn't approve of; it's the white I get from my daddy they don't like."

"What the hell?" Noah shouted.

"There's never been a mixed-race marriage in Malcom's family, and his parents are adamant that it stays that way. They can trace their family roots back to Jamestown. Anyway, that's why we fought and ultimately broke up." Sissy wiped the tears from her eyes and dropped the bomb.

"When the storm hit, and he thought I was here alone with Memaw, it made him realize how much I mean to him. He was afraid that he might have lost me forever, and he wants us to try again, Noah. I have to give us a chance. Please tell me you understand?"

Noah stepped away and saw the anguish on her face. "Make me understand," he said, trying to hold it all together.

"I love him, Noah," she answered, only this time with a smile. "I love him, I don't know what more I can say."

And there it was, the three words that Noah could understand. Because he, too, knew how it felt to be in love with someone and have huge obstacles to overcome. He had always known that Lottie wasn't going to return the feelings that he had for her, but if Sissy had a chance for a life with the man she loved, he wouldn't do anything to stand in her way.

The last few days had been the most meaningful he'd had, well, in pretty much forever, and Noah knew he would cherish them. But Sissy had to follow her heart and it was time he returned to the one girl who never let him down. *The Lark.*

So, he kissed her softly on the head and said, "I understand."

31

Now

It was uncomfortable being inside Shirlene's house alone with Sissy, but the sheriff had asked that everyone stay put until they could check out the damage. A few neighborhoods had lost their power and had downed lines, and the last thing anyone wanted was for someone to be hurt, or worse.

Noah tried to read, but even though he stayed awake this time, nothing was registering. Sissy pretended to watch TV, but when Noah looked her way, he could see that her mind was a million miles away. Finally, he couldn't take it anymore.

"Sissy," he said to her. "Are you feeling guilty for what happened between us, or is it something else?"

He could see the color creeping up on her face as he waited for her to answer. "I need you to know; I mean I want you to know that I don't take making love with you lightly. Malcom is the only other man I've been with Noah, and as much as I love him, and I do love him, it was never like that with him. I won't tell him that of course, but what if I never have those feelings again?"

Noah got up and sat beside her on the couch. "Sissy, I'm a little more experienced than you are, but what went on between us was pretty amazing and not like anything I've ever known, either. Maybe it was circumstance, maybe it was more, but I appreciate knowing that it meant something to you, too. I don't know your Malcom, and I defiantly don't want you to tell him about me, but give things time, and they'll work out. Sex isn't the most important thing in a relationship, but being able to please your partner sure helps."

"Please don't be mad at me, Noah," she said, tears threatening to fall from her big brown eyes.

"I could never be mad at you, Sissy," he said gently, and he realized that he meant it.

They were sitting there, arms around each other like old friends instead of lovers when Noah heard the horn honk. He looked out the front window and there sat Deputy Will, motioning for them to come out.

Noah grabbed his duffle bag and phone, and Sissy shoved her phone in her pocket, and they headed to the door. Rhett Butler had been out and was snoring by the stove, and Miss Scarlet was rubbing up and down Noah's legs. He stopped long enough to scratch behind her ears, but before opening the door, he pulled Sissy close.

"You're one hell of a woman, Sierra, and if I ever make it to New Orleans, I'm going to take you up on that drink."

Not giving her a chance to respond, he stepped through a puddle right into the sunshine.

When they got to the Bait Bucket, Noah knew that he needed to go and say goodbye to Shirlene, but he truly wanted nothing more than to stay in the cruiser and let Sissy become a special memory. But his good manners wouldn't allow it.

He thanked Deputy Will and opened the door to the restaurant. Shirlene and Sissy were laughing and hugging, and Noah was almost embarrassed to interrupt. But as soon as she saw him, Shirlene opened her arms, and he let her pull him in.

"Thank you for watching after my Sissy," she said. "I'd have been a wreck if she was home alone, and somebody needed to take care of the babies."

Noah looked at her face, with eyes so like her granddaughter's, and nodded. Something told him there was more going on than Shirlene was telling him, but that was going to have to be a story for another day. He still needed to talk with Andy and check on his boat, but more than anything, he needed to go home.

32
Now

Noah was nervous as he walked to the dock. *Had his boat survived the storm? Would he be even able to leave?* But as he approached, it was almost as if *The Lark* was calling to him. The moorings had loosened some as she'd been pushed around in the wind, but she was still there, and that was a huge relief.

After a visual inspection inside and out that showed some damage that he knew could wait, Noah cranked up the engine and was elated that it caught the first time. It was a good eleven-hour trip back to Anna Maria Island, but at this moment, he didn't care. He needed to get the hell out of Venice, Louisiana, and he wasn't sure that he ever wanted to come back.

As soon as he was underway, he sent a text to Pop that he was fine and was heading home. And because his phone was right there, he sent one to Stella, as well.

> *Wanted to let you know that I survived the storm and am headed home.*
> *Hope all is going well with you. Talk soon, N.*
> The response was almost immediate.
> *N? Which N is this?*
> *Ha-ha, very funny. I can't text and drive… see ya.*
> *Be safe N!*

For the first time all day, Noah relaxed and let the peace of the finally calm waters rush over him. He did his best not to think about Sissy; sometimes he was successful, and sometimes he wasn't, but mostly he was grateful for a glimpse of a life he never thought he wanted, but now knew that he wanted more than anything.

Before they'd left the house, Sissy had wrapped the last two sandwiches and packed them in Noah's duffle bag for his lunch. Shirlene had been out of beer and about everything else at the convenience store, so he'd grabbed three cans of cold orange soda from the store's cooler for the trip home and decided it was time to give one a try.

"Not bad," he said out loud, and turned *The Lark* towards Panama City, his layover for the night.

***

The damage from the storm had taken its toll here as well, and at first Noah was concerned about even stopping. But when he pulled up, someone came out immediately to show him where to dock, and it eased his fears. Yes, they'd been hit hard by the storm, but while the beach was a mess, the wharf and the landing hadn't received any real damage.

"Where can I get something that's quick and good?" Noah asked the deck hand who was helping him tie up *The Lark*.

The kid didn't look much past eighteen, and his idea of, "Quick and good" weren't exactly what Noah was looking for. The sly smile on his face was quickly dashed when Noah threw in the word dinner.

"I'm hungry," he told the kid. "I want someplace I can eat in peace and get in and out with no drama."

"The Pixie Diner is the place for you," the young man said. "Good food, fast, just like Mama used to make."

Noah chuckled, thinking the guy probably still ate dinner with his mama most nights, but he gave him a twenty for his help and headed in the direction of the diner.

After a huge plate of meatloaf, mashed potatoes, and a side of green beans, Noah was stuffed and ready to call it a day. The kid had been right, the food was good, but for him, growing up without his mother, it was like Pop used to make and still did.

There was some water on the deck inside *The Lark,* and his bed felt a little damp, but he didn't care. He brushed his teeth, changed into the sweatpants he had in his duffle bag, and climbed into bed, happy to be one step closer to home.

33
Then

Nick was patting his back, doing his best to get Noah to quit crying. At only two years old he couldn't understand why his world had been turned upside down, and he wasn't happy; he wasn't happy at all.

"Go home," he cried, looking at his brother while tears ran down his face. "Pop, 'I unt Pop," he continued until Nick started to cry, too.

The day Noah had come home from the hospital, Nick had become a big brother in more ways than one. Now they were living in New York City with their mom, in a small walk-up apartment, away from the sun and sand of Anna Maria Island, and all three Greyson kids were homesick. But Noah wasn't much more than a baby in Nick's eyes, and it was up to him to take care of him.

"Why are you guys crying?" Six-year-old Maya asked, scooting in between her brothers.

"Noah wants Pop," Nick tried to tell her, the tears rolling down his cheeks. "And I do, too."

"Pop, my Pop," Noah repeated, hoping he was getting his message across.

Maya shook her head. "I miss him, too." She said, trying not to join in the cryfest. "But this is where we live now."

She put her arms around her brothers and said, "It's okay, buddies, I'll take care of you." She started singing the lawnmower song that Pop always sang to them before bed or when they needed comfort. But when she reached the last stanza of "Oh how I love you," it was more than any of them could bear.

The day they'd left Florida for New York City, Pop had sat them all down and told them how much he loved them, and that home was wherever your heart was. He had also told them that his heart would always be with the three of them. He meant it to calm the fear he saw in his children's faces, but all it did was reinforce what they already knew. Home was where Pop was; and that was in Florida, on Anna Maria Island.

Seven years later the world was turned upside down again when their mother sent them away from her and back to their dad. Nick and Maya had reminded him of how hard it had been for Noah to leave Florida for their mother's home in New York, because after seven years away he couldn't remember his beginnings on Anna Maria Island. But once he was back on the island, living at the marina with Pop, Noah never forgot again.

34
Now

Noah was up the next morning before dawn, more anxious than ever to get back home. He chuckled when he realized that only a few days ago, he'd wanted nothing more than to get back out to sea, but the time in Louisiana and with Sissy seemed to have changed him. *Maybe it's time to take Pop up on his offer to help him run the marina,* he thought. *But then again, maybe his brain was just waterlogged.*

Pop and Nick were waiting for him when he pulled into the bay and helped him get *The Lark* settled into her slip. "From what I've been hearing on the radio, Louisiana provided you with a wild adventure. And from what I can see here on *The Lark,* she had one, too," Pop said, giving Noah a welcome-home hug.

Nick and Noah shook hands and the three of them looked over the boat. "It doesn't appear to have anything more than some cosmetic damage," Pop told them. "We need to check her out better tomorrow to be sure. Now how about a beer?"

Noah dropped his duffle bag on the deck and took the can of cold Coors from his dad. "Thanks," he said, plopping down in one of the big Adirondack chairs. "It feels good to be home and, better yet, to be out of Louisiana."

"So, tell us everything, little brother," Nick teased. "What was the most dangerous, the storm or the woman you met?"

Noah wasn't ready to share his time with Sissy yet, so he told them an alternate version, but one that was the truth. "Let's just say I rekindled with a woman I'd met before and leave it at that."

"Nothing doing," Nick told him. "You asked me how young was too young when you called, and now, I want details."

Pop was shaking his head when Noah answered. "Okay, since you asked, I had dinner with a woman I met the last time I was in Venice; Shirlene. She has the prettiest brown eyes, and she's tall and—"

"But how old is she?" Nick demanded. "Please tell me she's not jailbait."

Noah could hardly keep a straight face. "I could definitely take her out for a drink," he goaded his brother. "But as for her age, I'd say close to sixty."

Nick almost spit out his beer when he heard what Noah was saying. "Sixty!" he shouted. "You asked what was too young; surely you weren't talking about this Shirlene?"

"Seems to me you're awfully interested in my sex life, Nick. Don't tell me Lottie's cut you off already?" Noah laughed. "Do you need any pointers?"

"We're not here to discuss my life, Noah," Nick said sternly. "Just so you know, we're doing great."

"I haven't heard you two go at each other like this since you were kids," Pop intervened. "What's going on?"

Noah raised his hands in surrender. "There's nothing going on, Pop," he laughed. "Only some good old brotherly love, right Nick?"

"Whatever you say," Nick said under his breath as he stomped off the deck.

Pop didn't look convinced, but he didn't say another word. His sons were adults and, most importantly, the heckling had stopped.

"I would like to hear about the storm," he said cautiously. "We were all concerned about you."

Noah ran his hands through his hair and let out a deep sigh. "I appreciate that, Pop," he said. "I was pretty concerned myself, but thankfully, it all turned out okay."

"I take it this Shirlene was who put you up?" his father asked.

"Kind of," Noah said. "She's the owner of the town's only restaurant, gas station, and convenience store, and she has the only generator. She stayed in town to take care of some people without any place else to go and asked if I'd stay at her house and help with her pets." *And keep her granddaughter safe*, he thought but didn't add.

Nick happened to pick that time to join them back on the deck. "*Help* with the pets?" he questioned. "Now the story's coming out."

Noah loved his brother, and he'd asked him for advice, but that didn't mean he had to share everything with him. He also didn't want to have another argument, so he stood up, picked his duffle bag off the floor, and simply said, "Not yet it isn't."

Neither Pop nor Nick said another word as he went inside to unpack.

Noah laid his phone on his desk and stared at it. It hadn't occurred to him to ask Sissy for her phone number before they'd had to say goodbye, but it sure would be nice to talk with her right now. He'd left his number with Shirlene, and she'd given him the number to the Bait Bucket before he took Sissy home in the storm, but calling her there would raise questions that he didn't want either one of them to have to answer. And besides, she was in love with Malcolm, and he was going to respect that.

The clothes in his duffle bag were dank and dirty so they went directly into the washer. His Dopp kit had been inside the bag, and he didn't want to start harvesting mold or mildew, so he dumped everything out and assessed the damage. A new toothbrush and razor were cheap, so he threw the old ones away. His aftershave was in a plastic bottle, so it went in the keep pile along with the remaining condoms. Noah smiled, thankful that he'd been prepared and for the amazing two days he'd spent with Sissy.

He was trying to decide whether to feel sorry for himself about the situation when he heard the ding of his cell phone. The message he read brought a smile to his face, and he pushed Sissy to the back of his mind where he hoped she'd stay.

35
Now

Hey, N, you make it home yet?
Who's asking?
Cute, Greyson, you know exactly who it is.
The screen says Anonymous so how can I be sure?
You're right; you can't. Bye
Wait...; it's all coming back.

They texted back and forth until Nick knocked on the door and asked if he could come in. *Nick knocking?* Noah wasn't missing this.

Gotta run, but thanks for checking on me. Talk soon.

"Noah," Nick said again. "May I come in?"

Noah pulled open the door and gestured for his brother to enter the room.

"Since when do you knock," he asked.

"I don't live here anymore, and I wasn't sure. Plus, you seemed kind of pissed at me earlier, and I didn't want to take anything for granted." Nick looked so serious that Noah couldn't help but laugh.

"This will always be your home, Nick, well as long as Pop owns the marina anyway. And I wasn't pissed, but I have some things to work out in my mind before I talk about them. Can you understand that?"

Nick nodded. "I've been your brother for twenty-nine years," he said. "Don't expect that I can just turn it off and on. Especially when you asked for my help."

"I know I asked, Nick, and I appreciate all of your help, but for now you're going to have to trust me."

"I do, Noah, you know that. But if something changes, I'm here. Now on a less serious note, Pop says to tell you that dinner's ready."

"What are we having?" Noah questioned.

"You're having tacos," Nick laughed. "I'm going home to Charlotte's experiment of the day."

"Maybe you should have a taco before you go," Noah told him.

"I already have," Nick said, slapping his brother on the back.

"Except for the whole cooking thing, I'd say marriage agrees with you," said Noah, "But I need to ask you a personal question about your wife."

Nick's demeanor immediately became rigid. "Tread lightly, Noah," he said sternly. "She is *my* wife."

"But I just have to know," Noah continued. "After a lifetime of calling her Lottie, how can you call her Charlotte?"

"That's what you wanted to ask me?" he laughed. "Well, I wish I could tell you my secret, brother," Nick continued, and turned Noah's words back on him. "But for now, you're going to have to trust me."

36

Now

Sleep had been elusive the night before, and Noah woke up groggy and restless. He'd always liked his bed at the marina and always liked his bed on *The Lark.* So why was it that after two days in one filled with soft downy feathers, nothing else compared? Or, had it been the gorgeous curvy woman beside him that made the difference?

He rubbed the sleep from his eyes and decided to go ahead and get up. The aroma of freshly brewed coffee filled the air as he followed his nose to the kitchen. Pop was at the table, a big mug of his morning brew beside him, and the Bradenton Herald spread out on the table before him. It was a scene Noah had witnessed a thousand times, yet for some reason, it always made him feel secure.

"Morning, son," Pop said looking up from his paper. "Did you sleep well?"

Noah poured himself a mug of the fragrant brew, thankful that it wasn't laced with chicory. His automatic response was to say that he'd slept fine, but he decided against it. He took a sip of the hot coffee and sat down at the table.

"You think it's time I got a place of my own, Pop? I'm thirty years old and I'm still living at home."

Nicholas Greyson had missed out on seven years of his children's lives when their mother had whisked them off to New York, so as far as he was concerned, they could live with him forever, but only if that's what they wanted.

"Is that what you want to do?" he asked his son.

"I don't know, Pop," Noah replied, shaking his head. "These past few years I've told myself I lived on *The Lark* but stayed with you when

I needed a home base, but I'm not sure that's true anymore or if it ever really was."

"You were happy to head back out on the water when you left for Louisiana. What happened to make you so pensive all of a sudden? And don't tell me the storm because you've lived around the water most of your life and lived through storms worse than that one."

Noah thought about what he wanted to say. It was more than about Sissy and the connection they'd made, but he wasn't sure how to put it into words. He knew now that he wanted more, whatever that meant.

"I don't know, Pop," Noah told him truthfully. "Maybe I'm finally growing up. I can't imagine my life without *The Lark*, but I think I need more in my life than playing at being a sea captain."

That brought a smile to Pop's face. "You are a sea captain, Noah Greyson. That's all you've wanted since you were eighteen, but that doesn't mean you can't have stability in your life, as well. Whatever it is you choose; you don't have to decide today. You have a boat that needs some attention and an old man who's ready for breakfast."

"Thanks, Pop," Noah told him. "I needed to hear that. Now enjoy your paper because I'm cooking this morning. How about French toast? I made a batch while I was in Louisiana, and it was almost as good as yours."

While Noah cooked, the two men talked about the storm that he'd had encountered, the repairs *The Lark* was going to need, and Nick going back to school. After breakfast Pop helped with the clean-up and they discussed some changes he wanted to make at the marina, the possibility of a family dinner at *Stavros* with Maya, Dimi and the twins, and even the difference at Olde Florida Bank since Charlotte had left. But nothing more was said about Noah moving out or giving up his life on *The Lark*. It was a normal morning at the marina, and it was exactly what he needed. There really was no place like home.

93

37
Now

They spent the day working on *The Lark*, cleaning, scraping, and painting, even though Pop was tied up for a couple of hours working with the owner of a 2013 Outer Reefs yacht. It was a seventy-foot fiberglass beauty, and the client was looking for a place to store her for the winter. Noah knew if he had a boat like that, he'd take it and head to Fiji or some other warm, exotic location. Having those thoughts helped him relax about his future, and he decided that maybe his days as a commercial charter boat captain weren't over quite yet.

By evening they were both exhausted but pleased with the progress they'd made. "How about I run to Publix and pick-up some chicken?" Noah asked after he had showered. "I want nothing more than to sit on the deck with a cold beer and enjoy a supper I didn't have to cook."

Pop agreed and headed to his bedroom and a shower of his own.

Noah was waiting his turn in line at the store when two warm arms wrapped around his waist. "I thought you were leaving the island for a while," said the sexy voice behind him, and without even looking, Noah knew that it was Lindsey.

He turned around to face her and gently untangled himself from her grasp. "Lindsey," he said as politely as he could. "I did leave and made it as far as Louisiana before I ran into that tropical storm that went through. Ended up having to come back for some repairs."

"Why don't you forget that deli food and come home with me for dinner?" she unabashedly flirted. "I just stopped to get a steak to throw on the grill, but I can grab another one." She looked at him with such hope that Noah almost felt sorry for her, but there was no way he was going back down that road again.

"Sorry, Lindsey," he told her. "My Pop's waiting on me."

The hurt in her eyes was obvious, but she nodded and turned away. "Maybe another time," she called out, but all he could think about was how glad he was that he'd been honest with her after their tryst in his truck, and how fine her ass looked as she sashayed down the frozen food aisle.

Pop had everything set up on the deck when Noah arrived back at the marina and offered him a cold beer. "We worked hard today," he said, touching his beer against his son's. "Here's to a quiet evening and fried chicken!"

Noah spread out the containers of Publix famous Southern potato salad and hickory smoked baked beans that he'd picked up to go with the chicken, and for several minutes the only sounds to be heard were the ones from two men enjoying their meal.

"I wonder what Lottie's serving Nick tonight," Noah chuckled. "I don't know whether to be happy for him or not."

"Her cooking's coming along great," Pop said, reaching for a chicken breast. "I'm pretty sure there isn't anything Lottie can't do well if she puts her mind to it."

"That's good to hear," Noah answered. "Nick probably needs all the strength he can muster keeping up with her."

Pop raised his eyebrows, and Noah realized how what he'd said had sounded. "I didn't mean in the bedroom, Pop," he tried to explain. "But the Lottie I know isn't one to sit around and accept status quo; she always needs a project."

"You're right about that," Pop said, and thankfully the subject of Lottie was dropped.

After dinner they sat on the deck until the no-see-ums made it too miserable for Noah to stay outside. "Damn those bugs," he swore as he scratched at the painful bites on his leg. "You'd think we'd have learned by now to use some bug repellant at night."

"You mean like this," Pop asked, holding up the can of spray.

"Where did that come from?" Noah asked, trying not to dig at the relentless itching on his legs.

"Right here on the table by the slider," laughed Pop. "Just like it's always been."

Noah swore under his breath and left his Dad still laughing on the deck. He turned on the television, but there was nothing that interested him. Before he'd given up his freewheeling bachelor lifestyle, he would have grabbed his keys and headed to the Crab Shack, or another local hangout, but especially after running in to Lindsey earlier, he knew that would be a bad decision.

He decided that it'd been a long day, and maybe the best thing to do was stretch out on his bed and read until he was sleepy. The book he'd been trying to get into had already lulled him to sleep twice, and he had high hopes that it would again. But when he reached his room, the first thing he did was look at his phone, and there was a message from Stella.

Call me as soon as you get this. PLEASE.

38

Now

Noah found her name in his contacts and tapped it as soon as he read the message. But after four rings it went directly to her voicemail. "Hi, this is Stella," he heard, but hit end before letting the recording finish. Instead he tried the call again, only to receive the same response.

Shit! What should I do now? Keep trying, or wait for her to call or text? While he was contemplating his options, the phone rang, and he about jumped out of his skin.

"Stella?" he said without even looking at the caller ID.

"Sorry to disappoint you," the voice on the other end said. "But I am calling on her behalf."

"What's going on, Nick?" Noah asked his brother. "Did something happen to Stella?"

"As far as I know she's fine," Nick responded. "But I received a call from Senator Harper's assistant letting me know that Adam Jennings probably won't make it through the night. His family is there with him, but you know how hard this is going to be for Stella with the media circus that's going to surround her when he dies."

"She sent me a text to call her, but I didn't see it until just now. I've tried twice but she isn't answering. Damn it, Nick, where could she be?"

"If I know Stella, she's curled in a ball on her bed crying her eyes out," Nick told him. "She's like a little girl when bad things happen, and the whole fucking fiasco with Adam has been as bad as it gets."

"Is her mom going to her?" Noah asked.

Snarky wasn't a strong enough description of Nick's reply. "Seriously? If her mother would have been a mother instead of a senator when this mess started, it might have had a different outcome.

As it is, Stella's been left alone to deal with an attempted rape, stalking, and me being shot all from a former boyfriend. Senator Harper needed to pull her head out of her ass years ago and be a parent."

It took Noah a few seconds to put together everything Nick was saying. "I had no idea," he finally told his brother. "But I sure wish I had. Why didn't you tell me, Nick, when I told you about Stella coming to the marina?"

"Number one," Nick replied, "it was part of an investigation the FBI was handling, and I couldn't tell anyone. And two, because it was never my story to share. If Stella wanted you to know, she would have told you herself."

"Kind of like the FBI sting at the bank, Nick?" Noah spat back.

"That's hitting below the belt, Noah," Nick growled, "I had a job to do, and in both instances I was under sworn oath to keep quiet. If you don't understand that, tough shit. Now I've told you what I know because you seem intent on trying to be friends with Stella."

Noah was waiting for his brother to hang up on him, but he didn't. "Thank you for the call," he said curtly. "If I hear from Stella, I'll let you know, and I'd appreciate the same courtesy."

"Noah," Nick said again. "Be careful, okay? Kathleen Harper's a powerful woman, and you don't want to end up on her bad side. She wants the world to see her family as perfect, and all this mess with Adam Jennings has played havoc with that idyllic picture."

"I really am a grown-up Nick, even if you don't choose to believe it. I like Stella a lot, and I promise not to hurt her." Noah said the words but wasn't sure that he could back them up. He was serious about not hurting Stella, but being a grown-up? Even he wasn't sure about that.

39

Now

Noah tried Stella's cell three more times before she finally answered. "Hello," she said in a soft, tear-strained voice. It was like a knife to his heart.

"Stella, why haven't you answered your phone? I just talked to Nick, and I've been worried sick about you."

"My manager was here and wouldn't let me answer any calls," she told him. "But I'm alone right now. Have you heard about Adam?"

"Nick told me," he replied.

"I don't know what to do, Noah; please tell me what to do."

"The first thing is to tell me where you are," he demanded.

"In Miami," Stella said through her sniffling. "I have a big photo shoot tomorrow for one of the cruise lines, but I'm going to look like shit."

"Surely your manger can work out some kind of a reprieve for a couple of days. It's in their best interest if you're looking your usual stunning self, right?"

"But what about my interests, Noah?" she cried. "I want to go home, but Teddy says I have a contract to fulfill, and my mother doesn't want me anywhere near Tampa. So, tell me, please, I'm begging you."

Noah swore under his breath. He didn't really know much about Stella Harper other than what Nick and the tabloids had said. But he knew that he liked her, and she needed help. Without really thinking things through, he made a decision and hoped it wasn't one he would live to regret.

"Tell me where you're staying?" he said. "I'm coming to you."

For a moment there was nothing, and then she started to cry again. "You'd do that for me, Noah?" she asked between sobs. "You'd drop everything and be with me? No one has ever done that for me in my whole life."

"Tell me where you're staying, and as soon as we hang up, I'll throw some things together and be on my way." Noah hoped he sounded more confident to her than he felt because he was pretty sure the shit would hit the fan when his brother found out. Not to mention her mom.

"Are you sure, Noah?" she asked, and this time he thought he could detect hope in her voice.

"I'm sure, but the sooner we hang up, the sooner I can be on the road. Now please, tell me where you're staying."

He could hear her rummaging through some papers before she answered. "I'm at the Palms Hotel, and the address is 3025 Collins Avenue. I'm in the penthouse so you'll have to call, and I'll buzz you in."

"The penthouse?" Noah teased. "I forgot you were a celebrity."

The lift in her voice that he'd heard before seemed to drop when she replied, "What I am is alone, Noah, and I really need a friend."

"You have one, Stella, I promise you that. Now put some cold cloths on your eyes and lie down. I'm probably five hours or more away and there's no sense in you waiting up on me." Noah tried to sound stern, but he wasn't sure she was buying it.

"I'm sure Teddy will tuck me in so don't worry about that. Promise you'll be safe, okay?"

Teddy tucking her in. What the hell was that all about? Was Teddy the manager she'd mentioned? But he couldn't ask; instead he said, "I'll be careful; you be careful, too."

Noah hit the red button to end the call and looked at the time. It was almost ten o'clock and he knew the smart thing to do would be to grab a few hours of sleep and then head out at daybreak, but he knew he couldn't wait. He was too keyed up from the call, and besides, Stella was waiting for him.

The duffle bag he'd taken with him to Louisiana was still damp, but he knew there was an overnight bag somewhere in the storage closet. As quietly as possible he moved boxes around until he found the small suitcase and carried it to his room.

100

What to take was a question he didn't have the answer to, so he threw in a pair of jeans, two pair of shorts, and shirts that would go with anything. Then thinking about Miami and the gorgeous beaches, Noah grabbed his swim trunks and tossed them in, as well. His Dopp kit was still open on the dresser, but he realized he hadn't thought to pick up a travel toothbrush or razor when he was at Publix the night before. The bottle of cologne went into the empty leather bag, along with a plan to stop along the way for some new toiletries. He was about to pull the zipper closed when the pack of condoms caught his eye. Did he take them or not? Deciding that he was making this trip to help Stella, and not to hook up with some babe on the beach, he put the condoms in a drawer and away from temptation.

Now all that was left to do was tell his dad and call his brother. Going before a firing squad seemed less intimidating.

40
Now

Pop was sprawled out in his lounge chair when Noah went into the living room. He had the landline phone in his hand which said to Noah that his dad was talking to Shelly. He hated to ask him to hang up, but he was anxious to be on the road; and he still had to talk with Nick.

"Uh, Pop," Noah stammered. "I need to talk to you for a minute."

Pop said a quick goodnight to Shelly with a promise to call her soon. He hung up the phone and said to Noah, "It looks like you're going somewhere, but *The Lark* still needs some work to be seaworthy."

Noah ran his hand over his messy dark blond hair and shook his head. "I'm headed to Miami, but by truck, not boat. You remember the guy who shot Nick, Adam Jennings?"

"Like I could ever forget him," Pop said vehemently. "Surely he's still in a prison hospital and not in Miami?"

"He's still in the hospital, but Nick called earlier to tell me he probably won't make it through the night. Anyway, it's a long story that I don't have time to tell, but Stella's in Miami, and well, I'm going there to be with her."

"I guess I missed the part about you and Stella being involved. When did that happen?" Pop asked.

"There's nothing between us Pop, nothing except friendship, that is. But she needs someone right now, and I think it has to be me. Anyway, I can tell you more when I get back, but I really need to takeoff."

Pop nodded but asked the one question Noah was trying to avoid. "You've told Nick about your plans, right?"

"I'll call him once I'm on the road." Noah said. "If I call him now, he'll want to try and stop me, and I'm going, Pop, regardless of what he says."

"Nick spent a lot of time with that girl, Noah," Pop told him, "and I know he cares about her. But, you're his brother. All I ask is that you're upfront with him and you remember what all he's gone through this summer. Nick's finally healthy and happy, and he doesn't need to be worrying about you."

"You have my word, Pop," Noah said as he stopped to hug his father. "I'm trying to be a friend to Stella, the kind of friend that you and Nick have both shown me how to be."

Noah started his truck and checked the fuel gage. He was going to need gas soon, but nothing was open this late on the island. He knew he had enough to make it to Bradenton, though, so after entering the address that Stella had given him in the GPS, he took off. He could have used a cup of Bev's acclaimed dark roast coffee for the trip, but like the rest of Anna Maria Island, the Island Coffee Haus was closed.

The roads were ominously quiet as he headed onto Gulf Drive towards Manatee Avenue and Bradenton. Noah remembered his high school days when he made this trip, often looking for a new girl to hook up with. He wasn't proud of the boy that he'd been back then, but at least he'd never had to talk a girl into sleeping with him. Not that it made him feel any better now, but he'd never met with much resistance. It kind of scared him to think about girls like Stella, who'd tried to say "no," or worse yet, his ten-year-old twin nieces. He'd knock the crap out of any punk who tried to put the moves on Nikki or Steffi.

Right before the ramp to turn onto I-75, Noah pulled into a Shell station and filled up his Ford F-150. It wasn't *The Lark,* of course, but he had a long history with this truck, both good memories and bad. The latest one had been his adventure with Lindsey, and while it had been good while it was happening, it had also been the catalyst that had sent him down this path of redemption.

The road loomed dark ahead of him but there were always cars on the interstate. Noah turned on his favorite country radio station and set the truck on cruise. He was starting to relax when he remembered that he needed to call Nick.

"Damn it!" he said, smacking his hand against the steering wheel, but he'd promised his dad, and he wasn't going to let him down. At the next exit he pulled off and found the Golden Arches of McDonalds shining brightly and followed their light to an almost empty parking lot.

His phone showed the time as eleven thirty-five, and Noah was sure Nick was sound asleep. Either that or buried deep in the one-woman Noah would have settled down with years ago. But despite the time, he punched in his brother's name and listened to the ringing of the phone.

"What's wrong?" was the only thing Nick said.

"Always the G-man, huh big brother," Noah said, hoping to lighten the approaching conversation.

"Something had better be wrong for you to call me at this time of night," Nick snarled. "We were…, I have class in the morning."

Noah had a pretty good idea of what *we were* was, and he didn't want to hear it any more than Nick wanted to say it. He hadn't thought much about Lottie since his trip to Louisiana but realizing that had him thinking about Sissy. Why was it all his thoughts came back around to a woman?

"Noah? Are you there?" Nick questioned.

"I'm here, Nick, or actually I'm on I-75 headed to Miami. I'm on my way to Stella, and I thought you should know."

Nick swore and Noah heard Lottie giggle in the background. "You told me we weren't going to use that word around your wife anymore," Noah laughed. "Yet you seem to have a hard time letting it go."

"I'm tired and I'm pissed as hell at you, Noah, but I'm also kind of proud. I'm not sure you're the person Stella needs right now, but at least you're trying, and that seems to be more than anyone else wants to do. But stay in touch, okay? And promise me you'll stay under the radar."

"Well hot damn!" Noah laughed. "My big brother's finally proud of me. But what do you mean about staying under the radar?"

"Remember all those tabloid stories about Stella and me being engaged? She thought they were a publicity stunt her manger set up, but I always wondered if her mother wasn't behind it."

"Stella's mom wanted her to marry *you?*" Noah could hardly contain himself.

"Laugh now, but I think she thought it would be prestigious and look good for her career if Stella married the man who tracked down her stalker. Senator Harper is always searching for an opportunity to promote herself. Come to think of it, you probably aren't famous enough to be husband material for her supermodel daughter, so forget I said anything."

"Very funny, big brother but just as well," Noah replied. "I'm going there because Stella needs a friend, not because she's looking for romance. I need to get back on the road, Nick, but I'll stay in touch."

41
Now

It was four in the morning when he finally pulled into the driveway at The Palms Hotel, and Noah was dead on his feet. He'd always enjoyed driving down the Tamiami Trail but doing it in the middle of the night was a whole different experience. The road that said *old Florida* in his mind was lit up with neon signs on both sides of the road, but several of them had seen better days. It made him think of some of the classic television shows that Pop liked to watch.

As soon as he pulled up to the entrance, a valet was there to meet him even though there was little sign of life around the immense structure before him. Allowing the valet to take his keys, Noah looked over the shimmering tropical oasis and let out a low whistle. The Palms was designed for someone with Stella Harper's star power, and now that he was here, he wasn't sure what to do.

The concierge stand was empty, but two beautiful young women were at the front desk, and when one of them smiled at him, Noah walked towards her.

"How may I help you?" she asked, with teeth that shined like pearls and blonde hair framing a flawlessly tanned face. Noah was certain that good looks were one of the qualifications for working there, but he had never been one to turn away from a pretty face. Returning the smile, he replied, "I'm here to see Stella Harper. I believe she's staying in the penthouse suite."

And just like that the smile was gone and an ice queen stood in her place. The young women looked Noah up and down before saying a word, making him feel very uncomfortable and very out of place.

"I'm sorry sir," she said as curtly and professionally as possible, "but we don't give out any information concerning our guests. If you know someone staying at our hotel, they would need to alert us before we can allow you to go any further in the facility."

Noah had been snubbed before, and he even understood where the blonde bitch was coming from, but he was exhausted and hungry and not interested in putting up with any of her shit. Taking his phone from his pocket he called Stella's cell.

"Hey, I'm sorry to wake you up, but I'm at the front desk and they—"

He didn't even finish his sentence before the call ended, and the phone on the desk rang. The blonde was turning varying shades of pink as she spoke to the person on the other end.

"Yes, Miss Harper," she said. "Yes, Miss Harper. I understand and of course, I'd be more than happy to personally escort your guest to the penthouse. We'll be up right away."

Trying her best not to act chastised, the blonde stepped out from behind the desk and motioned for Noah to follow her. "Miss Harper said to order breakfast for you, so if you'll tell me what you'd like, I'll have it sent up."

Noah was feeling a little embarrassed at this point. He knew the woman was only doing her job, but man, breakfast sounded good.

"I'll have pancakes, crisp bacon, and two eggs over medium," he told her with a big grin on his face. "Oh, and a large glass of orange juice and coffee. Lots of black coffee."

The woman only nodded and led Noah to an elevator on the far side of the lobby. As soon as they stepped into it and the blonde had pushed the button, he realized that it only had one destination. The penthouse suite.

The minute the door to the elevator opened Stella jumped in into his arms with tears running down her face. "You're here, you're really here," she cried.

Trying to be as kind as possible, Noah untangled her legs from around his waist and gently placed her back on the floor. "Of course, I'm here, Stella," he smiled. "I gave you my word, and that's something you don't ever have to doubt."

A slight cough grabbed his attention, and Noah realized the hostess from the front desk was still standing there. "I sent a text to the kitchen with your guest's breakfast order Miss Harper," she stammered. "May

I order something for you as well, or is there anything else I can do for you?"

Without even hesitating, the tall willowy-thin supermodel replied, "I'll have whatever he's having, and his name is Noah. Noah Greyson."

42

Now

Their breakfast came immediately, making Noah appreciate once more the perks that came with being a celebrity. He knew there had to be a lot of responsibility as well and looking at the girl in the Hello Kitty pajamas, her eyes puffy and swollen from crying, he could tell there was also a lot of sadness. At least for the one scarfing down her pancakes like there was no tomorrow.

"You going to eat all that?" he teased as she added enough syrup to drown anything left on her plate.

"I have a high metabolism," she told him, shoving a bite of egg into her mouth. "I can't gain weight if I try."

Noah arranged his eggs between his pancakes and drizzled them with syrup. He'd never given much thought to his own weight, but he'd been around women for enough years to know that they were always watching what went in their mouths. He was about to take the first bite when he remembered the last time he'd had this breakfast, and suddenly he lost his appetite.

Damn it Sissy! he thought. *Get out of my head.* His heart was hanging by the proverbial thread, just as his feelings for the girl he'd met in a storm were, but he couldn't let them go any farther. Besides, he was here for Stella.

After a few bites of bacon and moving the pancake and egg mixture around, Noah put the fancy cover back over his plate and took a few sips of the now tepid coffee. He was hoping the caffeine would wake him up, but the events of the past two days were catching up with him. He tried his best not to yawn, but the harder he tried, the bigger the yawns became.

Stella put the last bite in her mouth when she looked up and saw Noah, his eyes dropping and his head sagging. "You poor thing," she said, setting her own plate aside. "You came all this way to be with me, and you have to be exhausted."

"I am," he admitted. "But I want to hear about you and if you've heard anything more about Adam. And your photoshoot, were you able to cancel it?"

"The last I heard about Adam was around one when my mom's secretary said he was holding his own. She promised to call if she heard anything else, and the only call I've had since then was yours. As for the photoshoot, it goes on as scheduled, but I didn't expect that to change. Now, make yourself as comfortable as you can and climb into my big, soft bed. I have hair and make-up in twenty minutes, so you might as well make the best out of the money that's being spent on this suite."

Noah could see the fourposter bed from the living area of the suite, and it did look inviting with sheer draping around it and pillows stacked high, but he was here for Stella, not to take a nap. He was ready to give her the reasons why it was a bad idea when the phone rang. Stella's face, which was normally as creamy as fine English china, turned a ghostly white as she lifted the receiver, but when the fear on her face turned to a radiant smile, he took a deep breath and relaxed.

"Oh my gosh, he made it!" she shrieked. "Even the doctors can't believe it, but Adam's vital signs are back to normal, and he's breathing on his own. It's a miracle, Noah."

Noah put his arm around her and gave her a hug, but he couldn't be as jubilant as Stella was. Adam Jennings had tried to kill his brother, and Noah would never forget how Nick had looked when he'd first seen him that awful night in the hospital. He wasn't wishing for Adam to die, but even if he did live, it had better be strapped to a hospital bed or back in a prison cell, because one thing was for sure, Adam Jennings was never walking free again.

"So, was that your mom who called?" Noah asked cautiously.

"Heavens no," Stella giggled, obviously overjoyed at the news she'd been told. "My mom only calls me if I've done something that she thinks might not look good for her. Other than that, her secretary Jan communicates on her behalf."

Noah couldn't imagine a worse life for a girl, or for anyone for that matter, but he did his best to keep his thoughts contained. "One of these days, I'd like to hear the whole story about Adam Jennings, but for now I'm happy that you're happy."

Stella chewed on her thumb. "Adam's done a lot of bad things," she said softly. "But I forgave him a long time ago. I have to tell him that, Noah, so he can't die; he just can't."

Stella took Noah's hand and guided him into the bedroom. "I need to shower and be ready when the wizards arrive, so please, climb into bed and get some rest. I'll be right next door if you need anything."

"The wizards?" he questioned, too tired to stop her from pushing him down onto the bed.

"They take this," she said running her hand over her face and hair, "and make me beautiful! See, wizards."

Noah shook his head, too tired to argue. What in the world had Kathleen Harper done to her gorgeous little girl that Stella thought she needed wizards to make her beautiful? When Stella shut the bathroom door, he pulled his shirt over his head but decided it was best if he left on his jeans. Boots off and lying on the floor next to his shirt, he climbed under the silky sheets and fluffy down-filled comforter and fell asleep the minute his head hit the silky, soft pillow.

43
Now

"We overslept, Stella!" came a shriek from another room of the suite. "Wake up!"

The door on the other side of the bathroom opened with such force that Noah sat up with a jolt. Standing before him was a woman of about fifty in a long old-fashioned style nightgown, and when their eyes connected, she screamed even louder than she had before.

"Oh, my heavens, Stella," she ranted. "What have you done? Your mother's going to kill us both!"

Expecting to see the supermodel curled up in the bed with the shirtless man, she pulled back the covers just as Stella walked in the room.

"What's all the fuss about, Teddy?" she asked innocently. And then seeing Noah, his hair disheveled, and his eyes only half open, she started to laugh.

"I was having my hair and make-up done in the main bathroom, and I let Noah lie down in my bed to rest. Obviously, I couldn't send him to the other bedroom since that's where you were. Anyway, Teddy, this is my friend, Noah Greyson. You remember his brother, Nick, don't you? And Noah, this is Teddy, my friend, manager, and gate keeper."

The minute Nick's name was mentioned, Noah saw the blush start creeping over the older woman's face. He believed Nick when he said Stella was like a sister to him, but now he wondered if like Stella's mother, this frumpy woman thought his brother was husband material for the supermodel. Or, possibly, she had the hots for him herself.

Stella gave Noah a soft smile to let him know everything was okay, and when he looked at her, a firecracker came out of nowhere and ignited in the pit of his stomach. He'd thought before that Stella had a gorgeous face, but she was too young and too thin for his tastes. The woman standing before him, however, was stunning, and she looked nothing like a skinny little girl.

The long plait of dark hair she'd worn earlier was now hanging in waves down her back, reminding him of a fountain of flowing chocolate, and her smoky gray eyes were smoldering; dark and mysterious. And when she looked at him, he swore she was looking straight into his soul.

But it was the red bikini that was his undoing. *Why the hell did I think she was skinny?* Noah thought. Her breasts were spilling over the top of the micro small bandeau top, and her legs were long and lean like those of a thoroughbred. But when she turned to pick up her robe and Noah saw the curve of her back, and the two orbs barely covered by what looked like a piece of shiny red dental floss, he pulled up the sheet and covered himself back up.

"We don't have time to discuss this right now but don't think I'll forget it," Teddy huffed. "Sorry if I scared you, Noah. I've just never found a man in Stella's bed before. Now we have ten minutes before the photographer arrives. I'll throw on some clothes and meet you in the lobby."

Teddy stormed out of the room, leaving Noah and Stella in an awkward silence. Noah spoke first. "Uh, sorry if I caused you any trouble," he said, trying to decide whether or not it was safe for him to leave the protection of the bed. "I knew my lying down was a bad idea."

He slipped on his boots and reached for his shirt when Stella moved his way. "I think it was a very good idea, N," she teased him. "You're ripped, Noah Greyson; how did I not notice that before?" Noah tried to keep his head down to hide from both the embarrassment and the pleasure he was feeling. The sun was barely up, and already this day was turning out to be a good one.

"I thought you were doing this modeling thing for a cruise ship?" Noah asked, slipping the shirt over his rumpled hair. "Why is the photographer coming here?"

"It is for the cruise line," she answered. "It's like a package vacation we're selling. Guests come here from the airport and stay overnight, and then the hotel takes them to the port the next morning.

113

At the end of the cruise, it's the same in reverse, only they go back to the airport. Today we're doing photos by the pool, and tomorrow we'll go to the Port of Miami. Cruising is a mega money maker."

The smile that had been on her face a few minutes ago was now replaced with one of sadness. It was obvious to him that Stella saw herself as nothing but a sales tool, but who wouldn't want to buy into whatever she was selling?

"Now that you know Adam is okay, I might as well head back home," he told her. But I'm glad that things worked out."

"What? You can't leave. I want you to see me work and since the news about Adam is good, I thought we could go to lunch and then shop for a wedding present for Nick and Lottie. Teddy will be fine with it once she hears Nick's name." Stella smiled. "In case you couldn't tell, she has a bit of a crush on him."

Noah shook his head. "And how about you, Stella? Did you have a crush on my brother as well?" he asked.

"Oh, for goodness sakes, no!" she replied with a saucy grin. "Nick is way too rule conscious for me, and besides, I told you he was lovesick for Lottie. Nick was like my big brother, and I really admire him, but despite what my mother and Teddy wanted, there was no chemistry between us. But I have to admit, he was easy on the eyes! Now, what's it going to be, N? Are you spending the afternoon with me or not?"

"Okay," he agreed, trying to digest how he felt about her comment on Nick's looks. "But as soon as you're done here, I need to find an affordable hotel. I'm certain after last night they wouldn't rent me a room even if I had a black card, and I'm going to need a decent night's sleep. So, give me five minutes and I'll be ready to go."

Stella nodded and left him alone, but as soon as he got into the bathroom, Noah remembered that he'd never picked up a toothbrush or razor. He ran his fingers through his thick dirty blond hair, and splashed cold water on his face, but the stubble was going to have to stay. Putting a little of the toothpaste he found lying by the sink onto his finger, he did his best to clean his teeth, and realized this was as good as it could get in five minutes.

When he stepped back into the living room, there stood Stella, a wide-brimmed straw hat covering her mane of dark waves and large

114

rhinestone sunglasses perched on her upturned nose. She looked exactly like a forty's pin-up girl, and he felt an immediate and intensely physical reaction. *What the fuck, Greyson*, he thought. *Get a grip.*

44
Now

Noah was absolutely mesmerized watching Stella in action. The frightened, insecure, young girl he thought he knew totally owned the photoshoot and had everyone eating out of the palm of her hand. It was obvious that the camera loved her and so, it seemed, did the people involved behind the scenes.

"Perfect Stella," the director called as she moved in and around the pool. Every time she posed, Noah heard the camera clicking away, and he knew the director was enjoying her performance as much as he was. That is until the two male models came onto the set.

He watched as Stella coyly sipped on a fruity drink in a tall glass while the men tried to get her attention. But when she stood up, and one of them grabbed her around the waist, he saw red, and it wasn't from her bikini. The guy was big and looked like a typical surfer with long blond hair and a physique like Adonis, and even though he knew it was all a performance, Noah felt as if he was getting a little friendlier than necessary.

When the director called for a twenty-minute break, both models immediately tried to move close to Stella, but she politely waved them off and headed his way. "So, what did you think?" she asked him sincerely.

"I think it was amazing; you're amazing, and I've honestly never seen anything like it in my life. You're a natural Stella," he told her. "If I didn't know it was an act, I'd totally be booking a cruise."

"Maybe you still should," she teased. "I can probably get you a discount."

"As great as that sounds, I have my own cruise ship, only on a much smaller scale," Noah told her. "Maybe someday you'll want to take a ride on *The Lark* and see what a real boat is like."

"Maybe I will, but right now, I need lots of water and a make-up touchup."

"You look beautiful just the way you are, Stella," he told her, and he meant every word.

"Thanks, N, I appreciate that, but for the cash they're paying me, I need to let them powder my nose when they want to." Her smile lit up her face and once again all Noah could think about was how different her professional persona was from her private one.

"You go do your job, and I'll wait right here," he told her, pointing to a chair on the sidelines. "And Stella, tell the muscle man with the shaggy hair to keep his hands off your ass. If he doesn't, I'm telling Teddy."

Her eyes opened wide in shock until she saw Noah's wink. "I'll do my best," she answered in a low sexy voice that he'd never heard before, and then she walked away; the ass in question causing quite a rise.

Two hours later the shoot was complete. After sitting in the sweltering hot sun, in clothes that were heading into their second day, Noah was totally rung out. He needed a shower and a gallon of something cold and refreshing to drink. And then Stella appeared, and everything seemed better.

"Son of a bitch," he chuckled.

"I hope that's not me you're swearing at," she said, batting her eyelashes for effect.

"Nope, just thinking out loud," he told her. "Are you done for the day now, or what?"

"I need to talk with Teddy, change, and then I want food! Thank God I'm not one of those models who has to live on water and crudité's"

"Crudewhat's?" he questioned.

"You know," she laughed, "rabbit food. Carrots and celery. My mom uses words like that, and I guess that one just stuck. But what I'm hungry for is a cheeseburger and fries. Does that work for you?"

Noah nodded his approval. "How about you go talk with your gate lady while I find an affordable motel. I need a shave and a shower before I'll let you be seen in public with me."

"Noah I can get you a room here with no problem. The production company will even pick up the tab. So come on, let's get this party started!"

He reached out for her hand to tell her why he couldn't stay at The Palms, and when they touched, he was sure he felt the shock of electricity, like when he used to shuffle his feet on the carpet and then touch his sister Maya's hand. Now he needed that motel room more than ever. It was surely lack of sleep and watching Stella prance around in that shiny piece of red nothing that had his body so tightly wound, because right now, he was thinking thoughts about Stella Harper that would definitely have him on her mother's hit list.

45

Now

Finding a motel in his price range wasn't as easy as Noah had hoped, but finally, a small place down the beach that wasn't totally out of line came along. It wasn't anywhere near the palatial digs that Stella was staying in, but it was clean, and they'd even had a sign offering to supply their guests with any forgotten toiletries. Disposable toothbrush and razor in hand, he climbed the stairs to his room on the second floor.

The water pressure in the shower could have been stronger, but it did the job and helped him to feel human again. After shaving and properly brushing his teeth, Noah tried out the bed. It wasn't home, or the soft featherbed from Shirlene's house, but it would do. With only a towel wrapped around his waist, he sat down, knowing he owed his brother a call.

Nick picked up one the first ring. "How's it going, Noah?" he asked. "I'm sure you and Stella heard the news about Adam Jennings by now? That's one young man with a will to live."

"Yeah, some chick named Jan called Stella this morning." Noah replied. "But Adam's still in a coma, right?"

"That's what I hear. It's a shit-ass miracle if you asked me," Nick answered. "So, how's Stella handling the news?"

"She's happier than I've ever seen her, Nick; it's like night and day. Her feelings for that guy have to be pretty complicated," he sighed.

"If you're going to be her new BFF, she'll get around to telling you, but anyway, when are you coming home? Pop needs your input before he starts working on your dinghy."

"You did not call my girl a dinghy, did you, big brother?" Noah laughed. "But I don't think you have to worry about me becoming Stella's best friend. She's different than I thought, and watching her model is like watching a sculptor mold clay, but being her best friend? Nah, that's not me."

"So, when are you coming home?" Nick asked again.

"I've paid for a night at a motel, and I'll head back in the morning." Noah sighed, not sure why the thought of going home was bothering him so much. "Anyway, I need to go. There's someone knocking at my door."

Leaving on the chain, he opened it just enough to see who was on the other side. A strange, tall woman with short blonde hair, tortoise rimmed glasses, and a blue jumpsuit covering her from neck to ankles stood there. It left Noah speechless. *Was this one of Stella's model friends*, he wondered.

"Apparently the security in this motel isn't anything like mine," the woman told him. "I saw your truck out front, and the reception desk guy gave me your room number without any questions. Now are you going to let me in, or what?"

Noah slipped the chain from the door and opened it just enough to look at the woman behind the voice. It sounded like Stella, but it sure didn't look like Stella. He was thinking of what to say when she pushed her way into the room.

"I hope you have something else to wear," she grinned, looking at the half-naked man in front of her. "Because I'm pretty sure there's a No Shirt No Shoes No Service policy at the restaurant I want to take you to."

Noah looked down at his half-covered body and groaned. "Who are you and what have you done with Stella?" he quizzed. "The girl I know wouldn't come alone to a man's motel room and demand to be let in."

"I didn't exactly demand to be let in; I asked nicely. And what you're looking at is my alter ego, Stacy. She's who I become when I want to go out in public without the camera crazies following my every move. Now," she added, brushing a wisp of blonde hair off of her face, "will you please put on some clothes because I'm starving!"

46

Now

He hadn't exactly been thinking of lunch in a restaurant with Stella when he'd packed, so Noah donned the best that he had. Khaki board shorts, a lavender polo, and flip flops were going to have to do. Besides, the girl in the next room, Stacy/Stella, whomever she was, looked more like a schoolmarm than a supermodel, so surely he would fit in to any a restaurant she had in mind. When she saw him, Stella roamed her eyes up and down like she was buying a side of beef. "Listen," Noah told her curtly. "We can go for fast food as far as I'm concerned. I came here as a friend, not arm candy."

"And here I was thinking you looked too good to be having lunch with Stacy," Stella smirked. "Whatever, I hope you're not ashamed of me. And by the way, lavender's a good color on you. I like seeing a man secure in his masculinity."

Noah opened his mouth for a retort, but nothing came out. "Come on," he told her, trying to gain control of the situation. He couldn't resist adding, "And for the record, my masculinity has never come into question."

This time it was Stella who was left speechless.

Neither of them said a word as they walked down the two flights of stairs. It was then that Noah realized how far from The Palms his motel actually was. "Surely you didn't walk here?" he asked.

"I took an Uber," Stella smiled. "I had him drive by every motel until I saw your truck. Good thing you still have the same one, because I was in trouble if you didn't."

He couldn't help but laugh as he led the quirky supermodel to his truck. After helping her in and turning the key, he finally asked. "Where to Stacy?"

She giggled and directed him a few blocks off the main drag to an old brick building covered with murals and graffiti. A colorful array of bougainvillea grew beautifully around the outside, and an old wooden plank took the place of a sidewalk. The weather-beaten Coca Cola sign out front read *Bongos.*

"You want to eat here?" Noah questioned, never believing for a moment that the daughter of a United States Senator, and a celebrity at that, would choose to eat in such a dilapidated old restaurant.

"You're not a snob are you, N?" Stella asked him. "This is my favorite place to eat in all of Miami, and maybe even the world. Come on," she said sliding out of the truck. "You'll love it. Anyway, I know Nick did."

"I thought you said you weren't interested in Nick," Noah said tersely.

"I wasn't; I'm not," she answered sincerely and gave him the saucy little grin that made his boys take notice. "You're not jealous are you, Noah?"

Was he? It was a question he couldn't even think about, so he did his best to clear his mind and let Stella pull him inside.

The restaurant was everything she had said it was and more. The ambiance was a mixture of Old Cuba and nineteen fifties soda shoppe eclectic, with all the charm and warmth that was missing from most of the restaurants he frequented. Well except The Bait Bucket that is, but chances were good it would be a long time before he stepped foot back in Louisiana.

The owner knew Stella the moment they walked in and with a knowing wink referred to her as Stacy. "And who is your guest today, Miss Stacy," he asked, pulling the chair out for her to sit down.

The gentleman was about sixty, so Noah couldn't tell if he was being friendly or flirty with the woman sitting across from him. He waited to see how Stella would introduce him and when she said, "This is my very dear friend, Noah," he realized that he was pleased.

"Since this is Noah's first time here, I'm going to order for both of us," Stella told the man without even taking one of the menus he was offering.

"Bring us one chili cheeseburger platter, one BLT burger with cheese platter, an order of fried plantains, and two chocolate malts." Seeing the look on Noah's face she added, "And a pitcher of sweet tea."

Noah ran his hand over his face. "Who's going to eat all that food?" he questioned. "I hope you don't think it's going to be me."

"Trust me, okay? I promise you; this is going to be the best lunch you've ever had and none of it will go to waste." She gave him that look he wasn't quite sure what to do with, so he nodded.

The two glasses of iced tea Noah drank were sweet and cold, and he was thinking about a third when waiters came from the back carrying large trays laden with platters piled high with something that had his nose twitching and his stomach growling.

Stella bounced up and down like a toddler as the waiters artfully spread the food out in front of them. It was a banquet fit for a boat load of sailors, and here he was with one supermodel, who he reminded himself, had a high metabolism.

Stella picked up the chili cheeseburger and took a bite, allowing the thick meaty topping to ooze from around the bun. "Oh my gosh," she moaned. "This is so good." She continued to um and oh over every bite, and all Noah could do is stare. If he was blindfolded, he'd swear this was a woman having one of the best orgasms of her life, and with a shock of surprise, it hit him that he wished he was the one giving it to her.

Stella stopped eating long enough to take a drink of her malt and saw that Noah was looking her way. "Oops! Sorry," she said wiping globs of chili from her chin. "When I'm hungry, I get carried away."

Noah picked up one of the fried plantains and smiled in awe at the lovely woman before him. Stella Harper was defiantly an enigma, and he sure was going to enjoy figuring her out.

"Here," she told him, putting the half-eaten burger in his hands. "You can finish this one, and I'll start on the other one." Without waiting for Noah to agree, she picked up the other sandwich and resumed the moans with the overtly sexual overtones.

When the last crumb of food and been devoured, and the last slurp of malt swallowed, Stella sat back, finally satisfied. "I told you it was good, didn't I?" she beamed, and Noah had to admit that she'd been right. He couldn't remember when he'd eaten such a huge lunch, maybe back in high school, but never with a sweet and sassy woman sitting in front of him.

"So now what, Stacy?" he teased her. "Since you're directing this afternoon's adventure."

"We're going shopping!" Stella announced, getting out of her chair. "I want to buy Nick and Lottie a really special wedding present, and you're the person to help me do it."

Noah groaned and reached for his wallet to settle the check. But when he tried to pay, the owner waived him off saying, "It's been taking care of."

Not wanting to make a scene, Noah escorted Stella to his truck without saying a word. When she tried to start a conversation, he cut her off.

"Just so we're clear," he seethed. "I may not be rich and famous, but when I take a lady on a date, I expect to pay for it."

He shoved the keys in the ignition just as Stella touched his arm and softly asked, "Was this a date, N? Because if it was, it's the first one I've had since my senior prom."

47

Now

They drove in silence as Noah tried to digest the words he'd just heard. He wasn't one hundred percent sure how old Stella was, but he knew she couldn't be more than twenty-three, twenty-four, tops. And she hadn't had a date since she was what, eighteen? How could that be? She was a Sports Illustrated cover model, for heavens sakes.

All of a sudden Stella yelled, "Here! Turn here!"

Noah all but wrecked his truck trying to make a sharp turn into the parking lot, but when his breathing was back to normal, he turned in Stella's direction, the look on his face not one of amusement.

"You realize you could have gotten us killed back there, right?" he demanded.

Sheepishly, she pointed to the lavish building in front them and pointed. "But look, Noah, they have a Saks Fifth Avenue here. Can you think of any place more perfect to find exactly the right present for the newlyweds?"

He shook his head, having a hard time staying angry with her. "To be honest, Stella, I've never given it much thought."

"Well what did you give them?" she questioned.

"Was I supposed to give them something?" he retorted. "I went to the wedding, even bought a new suit and was the best man. You're saying I needed to buy them a gift, too?"

"Oh, N," she laughed. "You really need a woman in your life."

My sentiments exactly, he thought. *But maybe not for the reason you're thinking.*

Stella pulled him through the palatial building, cooing over stylish handbags from Gucci and Louis Vuitton, all with price tags that equaled more than a common man's weekly wage. When they finally made it to the department filled with fancy sparkly things, Stella went into all-out shopping mode.

"Do you think crystal or silver?" she asked, biting gently on her bottom lip.

"I have no fucking idea," he chuckled, deciding he liked looking at her mouth a lot more than the fluff inside the store.

"Come on," he finally said. "Let's go to *Bed, Bath and Beyond* and buy them some towels or something. Isn't that a normal wedding present?"

If his comment even registered, Noah never knew because Stella had her eye on something, and she was honing in. "We'd like to see that Baccarat crystal decanter set, please," Stella told the curvaceous bottle blonde behind the counter.

The woman was giving Noah lots of flirty smiles and eyelash batting but was paying no attention to the almost frumpish customer asking for help. On an ordinary shopping excursion, he would have enjoyed the attention, and probably even flirted back, but today he was having none of it.

"Honey," he said taking Stella's arm, "I really think the silver service we saw at Tiffany is better suited to the couple. Let's order it and have it shipped to them."

Stella was totally confused, but the blonde was not. Seeing that she was about to lose a sale, her demeanor changed immediately.

"Please, let me get that out for you," she said, trying not to blow her commission. "I apologize for not hearing you before, but my mother's ill, and she's all I can think about right now."

Noah knew she was feeding them a crock of shit, but it seemed to appease Stella. He stepped back and let her continue.

"It's exquisite, don't you think, Noah?" she asked, turning the cut crystal in her hands.

"Whatever you say, my love," he replied, and then casually put his arm around her and squeezed. *Too much*? He wasn't sure, but the look in Stella's soft, gray eyes when they met his own made him doubt the act he was putting on.

"We'll take it!" she exclaimed to the associate, and for a moment everyone was happy. And then Stella remembered her alias of Stacy, and that her credit cards would be in the name of Stella Harper. She looked at Noah and swallowed, and he shook his head.

Fifteen minutes later they were back in his truck, a beautifully wrapped package in a Saks Fifth Avenue Bag on Stella's arm, Noah's credit card balance increased by five hundred dollars, and her hand snuggly held inside of his. It had been the best shopping experience of his life.

48
Then

"We need to go shopping for a Father's Day present for Pop," Maya told her brothers. It was the first one they had shared with their dad in years, and the three Greyson kids wanted to make it special. "I have twelve dollars from babysitting last weekend; how much do you guys have to contribute?"

Nick proudly laid down the twenty-dollar bill that he'd earned from mowing the grass around the marina, and then two sets of eyes turned to Noah.

"Why didn't you tell me before that we were going shopping today, and I'd have saved my allowance? Five bucks a week doesn't go very far you know." Noah stuck his hands in the pockets of his shorts and grumbled. It wasn't his fault he didn't have a way to make extra money like Maya and Nick did, was it? Afterall, he was only nine years old!

"But you knew Father's Day was coming up, Airhead," Nick said, giving his brother's arm a punch. "What did you think we were going to do?"

Noah was embarrassed and a little bit ashamed. When they lived in New York with their mom, her husband Hudson had always bought a box of her favorite chocolates and put their names on the card. It hadn't really occurred to him that they needed to be responsible for a gift for Pop.

Nick turned away from Noah and asked Maya, who was the oldest, what she had in mind.

"It has to be something from a shop here on the island," she told them. "Someplace we can either walk or get to by the trolley. Maybe some cologne or a tie, that's what dads usually get for Father's Day. What do you think, Nick?"

"That doesn't seem like Pop," Nick told her. "He doesn't go anywhere to wear a tie or cologne. What about a new fishing pole? Pop loves to fish."

Maya agreed it was a good choice, and they walked together to the corner to catch the free Island Trolley. The hardware store in the shopping center was the perfect place to look for a fishing pole for Pop. Even though he had no money to contribute, Noah was excited thinking about the look on Pop's face when he opened his gift.

Unfortunately, none of the fishing poles in stock were for deep sea fishing or in their price range. The manager said he could order them something, but it wouldn't be in for two weeks, and Father's Day was Sunday.

They left the store dejected, and even though Noah was feeling the blame, neither Maya nor Nick came right out and said anything. They walked through the other shops, hoping the right gift would jump out at them, but it never did.

Noah never forgot that Father's Day. They'd ended up making homemade cards and fixing their dad a dinner of grilled hotdogs and chips, and Pop seemed genuinely thrilled. Even after he told them that having his kids back with him was the best present he could ever have hoped for, Noah held on to the feelings of guilt and never enjoyed shopping much again.

49
Now

"Noah," Stella started, when they were both in the truck and the A/C was running.

"Me first," he told her, looking directly into her eyes. "Would that salesclerk ever treat Stella Harper like she did you just now?"

She looked away and shook her head. "No, she'd have been all but kissing my feet."

"Then why did you let her treat Stacy like she did? Because she was a condescending bitch, and you allowed her to be."

"But Noah," Stella argued. "She didn't know it was me; she just thought I was some rich dumpy woman with a hot guy on her arm. It wasn't until you put her in her place that she changed her tune."

"My point exactly. No woman, no person, should ever be treated as if they're not worthy. You went into that store to drop some real cash on a gift, and you were excited about it, and she should have been, too. It shouldn't matter what you look like, or what your name is. Everyone deserves the same courtesy, and you should have been given it."

"Where did you get all this wisdom, Noah Greyson?" she asked him with a smile. "I don't think anyone has ever stood up for me the way that you did today, and I find it very sweet and very charming."

"I'm certain no one has ever used the words sweet and charming about me in a sentence before," he laughed. "But I learned this from watching Lottie. Mean girls, like the snooty clerk at Saks, treated her terribly when we were kids, but she always held her head high and never retaliated. At a party after she and Nick graduated from high school, one of them did something so ugly and hurtful that Lottie was not only humiliated, but her self-esteem was destroyed. She ran away from home and from Anna Maria Island to keep from dealing with the pain, and it broke the hearts of everyone who loved her."

"The Lottie I met seems like a strong, confidant woman. What made things change?"

"She stood up for herself when my brother fucked up, and despite what happened in their second go round at a relationship, it was good for her. Nick's pretty imposing when he's in full FBI mode, but Lottie held her ground and sent him away." Noah's face went soft as he remembered the events of that weekend; the one where he'd finally admitted to her how he felt.

"You care for her very much, don't you?" Stella asked softly.

"I do care for her," he answered honestly, and for the first time in a long time, he realized that the feelings he had for Lottie had changed. She would always be his first love, but that chapter of his life was closed, and he was finally ready to start a new one.

"Can I ask you one more question before we go?" Stella asked.

"Okay, one more," he grinned.

"Where in the world did you come up with that line about Tiffany and the silver service? I could hardly keep a straight face, and I thought the poor girl was going to pee her pants!"

"Something else I learned from my new sister-in-law," he chuckled. "Nick took her there to buy their wedding rings when they got to New York, and I overheard her telling Maya all about it. The name kind of popped in my head, and I ran with it."

"It worked out well for me," she smiled. "And for Lottie, too. What a lovely thing for Nick to do."

"Lovely?" Noah choked. "I think it's kind of sappy myself. He should have just thrown her over his shoulder and taken her to the justice of the peace. That's how I'd handle a woman who had my nuts all up in knots for years."

Stella shook her head, "Oh, N," she said, giving him that look that made him feel things he knew he shouldn't be feeling. "What am I going to do with you?"

They listened to the radio and made small talk and pulled up in front of Stella's hotel much faster than he would have liked. She'd already told him she had a business commitment that evening, and even though she asked him to stay another day, Noah said no.

"I need to go home and help my Pop with the repairs on *The Lark,*" he told her. "But I've had a really good time with you today. Who knew you had an alter ego?" he teased.

Stella took off the glasses and pulled the wig off of her long dark hair, shaking her head to let her silky locks flow naturally. "I had a good time, too," she answered. "One of the best I can remember in a long time. Thank you for coming to my rescue, Noah Greyson. You are now officially my knight in shining armor."

He leaned down to give her a sisterly kiss on the forehead, but Stella beat him at his own game. Using both hands, she took hold of his face and lifted her lips to his for a soft, warm kiss. And it was anything but sisterly.

50

Now

Now that he was alone, Noah realized how much he missed having Stella by his side. He really had enjoyed the day with her and was sorry when it had to end. But it was for the best, he told himself, especially when he thought about that kiss. It wasn't a kiss that said, "Let's go to bed," but somehow that made it more intimate, more erotic, and definitely more perplexing.

After the huge lunch, Noah decided to skip dinner and grab a beer at the bar. It was still early, so the crowd was slim, but that was fine with him. He was looking for liquid relaxation, not physical.

About halfway through his tall Blue Moon, a willowy brunette in skintight black jeans and a sheer white, off-the-shoulder blouse sat down next to him. She smiled and he smiled but then turned back to his beer.

"Are you one of the models with the cruise line?" her smooth as whiskey voice asked him.

"A model, me? No, I'm here visiting a friend," he laughed, catching himself before saying he was a friend of one of the models.

"Oh, so is your friend joining you?" she continued to pry.

Noah took a long pull on his beer and thought about the situation. He was tired, but horny and confused as hell. The woman beside him was gorgeous. He felt certain she'd know how to show him a good time, but his head was swimming with visions of the two women he'd spent time with recently, and he wasn't ready to give up on finding the right someone he could enjoy both in and out of bed.

Finally, he answered. "Not tonight," he told her. "But I wish she was." The bartender handed the woman something pink in a martini glass, and Noah went back to his beer. When he didn't try to pick her up or even engage in conversation, she took her drink and moved on.

Halfway into the second beer, he was starting to unwind when like a ton of bricks, it hit him. He *liked* Stella. Like really liked her, and he really liked Sissy, too, but neither one of them was available. Sissy was in love with Malcom and a relationship with Stella? The obstacles were too many to count.

He finished his beer, settled his tab, and headed to his room. Maybe he'd see things differently after a good night's sleep.

The room was dark when he entered making the flashing red light on the phone by the bed stand out like a sore thumb. He picked it up immediately, wondering why anyone would have left him a message there instead of on his cell, but the minute he heard the recording he understood.

"Hey, N, this is Stella," it began. "I just wanted to thank you again for such a wonderful day and to tell you goodnight. I'm not sure I can put into words what you coming to Miami meant to me, but it was a turning point in my life, and I'll never forget it. We're leaving before dawn tomorrow morning for the photoshoot on the ship, so please drive safely and send me a text when you get home. "

He listened to the recording twice just to hear her voice. *Damn it!* He could not develop feelings for Stella Harper. She was young and fragile and a celebrity supermodel with a United States Senator for a mom. He was the owner of a charter boat who still basically lived at home with his dad. He was not the man for Stella. He knew that, so why was his heart trying so hard to change his mind?

After a shower, this one with a little more water pressure, he brushed his teeth and laid out the clothes for his ride home. Everything else was thrown in his suitcase along with the memories of the past day.

He was too tired to watch television, and the beers were starting to slosh in his stomach, so he climbed in bed. The sheets weren't silky, and the bed was hard, but despite the thoughts going around and around in his mind, Noah closed his eyes and slept until morning.

51
Now

The trip home was long and boring. He'd hit the road around seven and stopped at a Waffle House for breakfast. Now there was nothing but pavement, cars, and hot sun before him. Early fall in Florida, especially southern Florida, was still hot and muggy, and Noah was thankful for the A/C blowing cool air into the cab of his truck.

Shortly after one thirty, he pulled into the marina parking lot, glad to be home. He'd truly enjoyed his time in Miami with Stella, but he appreciated water and sand without all the commotion of a place like Miami. *One more reason why they didn't stand a chance,* he thought.

Noah dropped the suitcase on his bed and made a mental note to start some laundry. Right after he said *hello t*o his dad and grabbed a sandwich and a cold drink.

"Hey Pop," he called out to his dad. "I made it home safe and sound."

"Good to know," Pop chuckled. "How was Miami? I heard from Nick that the Jennings' boy rallied again. How did Stella take the news?"

"She was very relieved," he told his dad. He really wanted to tell him about watching her work, the great lunch they'd had, and even the shopping expedition, but Noah decided it was something he needed to keep to himself.

Remembering that the wedding present for Nick and Lottie was still in his truck, he ran out to retrieve it before making lunch. It wasn't as if theft was high in their area, but no sense tempting fate by leaving five hundred bucks worth of snazzy glass lying around.

"I'm going to fix myself a sandwich," Noah added. "Can I fix something for you?"

"Whatever you're having will be great," Pop answered, wiping the sweat from his forehead. "And maybe some lemonade? I made a fresh pitcher this morning."

Noah loved the old kitchen in the living quarters of the marina and had balked when Pop had suggested remodeling it. Everything looked exactly the way it had when they'd moved back to the island from New York, and he didn't ever want to lose that memory. It had taken him some time to remember it, but this was home.

After fixing a lunch of meatloaf sandwiches, kosher pickles, and glasses of Pop's secret recipe lemonade, Noah took the food to the deck where his dad was already waiting.

"So tell me, what we need to do to *The Lark* to get her good and seaworthy?" Noah asked picking up his sandwich. "I've decided to stay around AMI and do some day excursions instead of looking for another tournament. You okay with that?"

"I've told you before that this is your home for as long as you want it, and besides, I like having the company."

Noah looked at his dad and smiled before asking the question that had been on his mind for a long time. "Pop," he started slowly. "I've never really known you to date, and until Shelly, I've never seen you interested in a woman. Well, besides mom that is. So how did you do it? Didn't you get... lonely?"

"Consciously, I know that I'm sitting here talking to a grown man, but inside I still see the teenage boy who came to me with questions about girls and condoms," Pop smiled. "That was a day I'll never forget. But to answer your question, when I was raising you kids you were my whole world, and I put my needs on the back burner. Doesn't mean I didn't find some female companionship from time to time, but I kept all of that away from here and from my family."

Noah looked at his father and knew that Nicholas Greyson, Sr. was one in a million. He'd given up everything to make sure he and Nick and Maya had a good, secure home, and he wondered if he knew how much his kids admired him.

"I love you, Pop," Noah said out of the blue, choking back his emotions.

"I know you do, son," Pop answered. "And I love you, too. Men may not think it's macho to say those words to anyone but a woman, but they're wrong. When you love somebody, you show it and you say it, regardless of who they are."

With a small smirk Noah asked, "So how about Shelly, Pop, do you say those words to her?"

52

Now

Pop never did answer his question, leaving Noah to wonder about the lovely nurse who had come into their lives when Nick had been shot, but he knew he'd tell him when there was something worth talking about. His dad had been alone a long time, and so had Shelly from what he'd heard. Apparently neither of them seemed to want to rush into anything.

It was too late in the day to start working on *The Lark*, so after cleaning up from lunch, he decided to take Nick and Lottie their wedding present. Leaving a breakable and expensive gift at the marina around two men, seemed like an accident waiting to happen.

When Noah went in search of Pop to let him know his plans, he found him stretched out in the backyard hammock talking to Shelly. *Why, you dog*, he laughed but decided to leave him in peace. His dad deserved to find someone after all these years, and he knew Nick and Maya were rooting for Shelly exactly like he was.

Lottie's little pink cottage on the beach looked the same as it had since she'd come back from Indiana. Buttercups and periwinkles preened in the afternoon sun as if they didn't have a care in the world, and shells of all different varieties and sizes gave them a quaint, seaside border. He knocked on the door, expecting to hear his brother hollering for him to come on in, but instead, Lottie pulled the door open and smiled at him.

"Noah," she said, pulling the door aside for him, "Come in."

As soon as he was in the doorway, Noah was hit by a terrible sense of déjà vu. He'd come here the day after Lottie had been let go from her job at Olde Florida Bank; the same day he finally admitted his feelings for her and the same day that Pop had called with the news about Nick being shot. And apparently, she felt it too, because the tension between them was thick enough to cut with a steak knife.

"Uh, is Nick here?" he asked, handing Lottie the beautifully wrapped gift.

"This is his late day at school," she answered, turning to the package in her hands. "What's this?"

"Stella wanted to give you a special wedding present, so this is kind of from both of us. Not sure Mom would think that's appropriate, but we picked it out together so…"

By now Lottie had the package unwrapped and was pulling the elegant decanter and two small glasses out of the box. "Oh, Noah!" she exclaimed. "It's exquisite. I saw one similar in New York, but Nick would have had a fit if I bought it. It's called a honeymoon decanter, and I fell in love at first sight."

Seeing Lottie light-up like this made Noah smile. He only wished Stella could have been here to see it, too. He followed his new sister-in-law onto the lanai where she placed the crystal pieces on a small cabinet that he knew had belonged to her gran.

"Your gran would be happy seeing you like this, Lottie," he told her gently. "I know it took you and Nick a long time to find your way back together, but I think you both have your happily ever after."

Lottie had tears in her eyes when she threw her arms around one of the best friends she'd ever had. "I think so too, Noah," she told him. "I think so, too."

The sound of a throat being cleared, much louder than necessary, interrupted the moment, and Noah pulled away knowing that his big brother had arrived home. But when Lottie rushed into the arms of the former FBI agent, the scowl on his face turned to nothing but love.

"Look what Noah brought us," she said, pulling Nick towards the antique chest. "Isn't it gorgeous?"

How anyone could stay upset with Charlotte Luce was beyond him, and apparently his brother thought so too, because Nick smiled and nodded at his wife's animation, and even gave Noah a quick thumbs up.

The admiring of the crystal complete, and Nick's summary of how his day had gone answered to Charlotte's satisfaction, Noah asked a question.

"So where can I go around here to meet a nice woman," he asked. "You know, someone not like anyone I've ever gone out with before."

Nick snorted and Lottie almost giggled at his analogy. "I guess that leaves all the bars out," she teased. "Maybe church?"

"Not a totally bad idea," Noah admitted, "but I don't want to wait until Sunday. I need to put myself out there now."

"What happened in Louisiana that has you in such a hurry to meet a woman? Correction; nice woman, Noah?" Nick asked. "I know there's something you're not telling us."

Noah sighed, deciding it was time to come clean about Sissy. "Believe it or not, I did meet someone in Louisiana, and I wasn't even looking. She's smart and beautiful, sassy and funny, and I'd have liked to see where it might have gone; problem is, she's in love with another guy."

Even Nick had a forlorn look on his face, but it was Lottie who spoke. "I'm so sorry, Noah," she told him. "We're both sorry. Do you want to tell us about her?"

"Nah, it won't change anything. That's why I'm looking for help."

While Lottie was thinking, Nick chimed in. "While we're waiting for my wife to find you a suitable woman, tell me about Miami and how Stella's getting along."

Tell Nick about Stella? That was worse than talking about Sissy, but thankfully he didn't have to.

"I've got it!" Lottie said, jumping up. "The Book Nook is having a book reading and signing tonight for B.B. Swann. She has a new book out, and I'm sure the flyer said romance. Nothing brings a group of women together like a hot new romance novel."

Problem solved? Hardly.

53
Now

What in the hell do you wear to a book reading? He knew the dress code for the island nightlife, but for a book reading? Not thoroughly convinced that this was the right thing to do, Noah searched through his closet looking for something that said, "Nice guy looking for nice girl." He laughed, thinking it sounded very much like a dating site profile.

The thing was, he wasn't certain he even qualified as a nice guy, at least when it came to women. Sure, he was *nice,* but he'd been around the block more than a few times, and maybe the vision he had in his head for a lady in his life wouldn't find that an appealing quality.

Finally, he decided on a pair of khakis and a blue and white pin striped oxford cloth shirt. He thought it gave him that businessman vibe he'd seen on Lottie's ex-boyfriend, Peter. The guy had been a tool, no doubt about that, but he was an attorney and dressed well—the only point in his favor.

Noah showered and shaved, knowing that he needed a haircut, but there wasn't time now. A spray of Versace Eros for good measure and it was time to dress.

The first thought that came to mind when he looked in the mirror was that he wished he was taking Stella out for a nice dinner. Not someplace that required a suit and tie but a restaurant that they both would be comfortable in. But that wasn't in the cards which is why he was going to a book reading looking like a yuppy or at least, what he thought a yuppy looked like.

Noah rolled up the sleeves of his shirt, showing off his deep summer tan and strong forearms and slipped into a pair of boat shoes.

"It's now or never," he sighed, and went in to say goodnight to Pop.

"You must have a hot date," his dad teased. "Who's the lucky girl?"

"I wish it was that simple," Noah replied. "Actually, I'm headed to The Book Nook in search of the perfect woman. Lottie says there's a romance author speaking tonight, and it might be a good place to find one."

Pop rubbed his chin, searching for the right words. "You know, son," he began. "It seems to me that women and love just come along; they're not something you can orchestrate. Go to this book thing if you think it will make a difference but go for fun and not with high expectations."

Noah nodded, not sure he had an answer to the wisdom his father had provided. What he wanted, what he *needed*, was a woman to help him get his mind off of Sissy and Stella, and tonight he was placing all his hopes on The Book Nook.

Lottie had suggested he arrive late so he would have to take a seat at the back, allowing him a good view of the women in front of him. He thought it was an ingenious idea, so he waited until five after seven to enter the store, and Lottie had been right! All the seats were taken by women of every size, shape, and hair color, and although he couldn't see faces from where he was sitting, he felt as if he'd walked into a goldmine of women.

Lydia Wells stepped to the front of the room and held up a bright yellow book as she introduced the author, B.B. Swann. Noah remembered seeing the joined hands on the book's cover, one definitely light-skinned, and the other one dark, and that made him stop to think about Sissy, and her situation with Malcom's family. It was because of those thoughts that he missed the beginning of the author's talk; the part where she said that *Breaking The Barriers* was a young adult romance novel.

Noah liked to read, but mystery and suspense were his favorite genres. He sat politely, pretending interest in the love story being discussed until the group was applauding, and the book signing began to get underway. One by one the women stood up from their chairs, and *Holy shit!* Most of them were girls! Teenage girls.

What the hell? Lydia Wells came up beside him and smiled. "What a surprise to see you here tonight, Noah," she said. "Are you looking for books for your nieces?"

A book for the twins? They were only ten years old, not YA, whatever that was. There was no way he was going to ever buy a book about love for the girls! *No way in hell!*

"Not for my nieces," he stammered. "I have a friend I thought might be interested."

It was certain that Mrs. Wells wasn't buying his story, but she nodded graciously and moved on. A couple of the girls had their mothers with them, and Noah could see at least one of them was looking at him a little too closely. Did she think he was a dirty, old man, or was she a lonely mom looking for some action? Whatever she was thinking, he wanted no part of it, so he stepped in line and waited to buy a book.

When it was his turn and Ms. Swann asked who he wanted the book signed to, he said the first name that came into his head. "Sissy. Sign it to Sissy."

She handed him the book, thanked him for coming, and Noah left the store as quickly as he could. Thinking about murdering his sister-in-law, and the fact that at the rate he was going he might never feel a soft warm woman beneath him again, he climbed into his truck and headed home. Alone again, naturally.

54
Now

The next few days went by quickly as he and Pop put all their free time into the repairs on *The Lark*. Pop had pulled her in to drydock while he was in Miami, so at least they weren't out in the hot sun all day. The work was tiring but satisfying, and most importantly it helped keep Noah's mind off women. Or worse yet, his lack of one.

Nights were the hardest. He was used to hitting the bars after dinner, sometimes to play pool with the guys but usually to try to talk his way into a pretty girl's bedroom. Those weren't options now. Sure, he would have enjoyed a game of pool and a cold beer on tap, but he knew that would only lead him back down the road he was trying to escape from.

So, he watched television and took lots of cold showers and even read some, but nothing was helping the ache in his heart or his groin.

Pop was having dinner in Tampa with Shelly and was going to spend the night in Tarpon Springs with Maya and her family, leaving Noah on his own. He'd spent many nights alone in his childhood home, but for some reason, tonight he felt nervous and fidgety. There was nothing on TV he wanted to watch. He'd finally finished the John Sanford novel he'd been reading and had already taken a very cold shower.

Not able to take the silence any longer, he picked up his phone, knowing he would be sorry later, and punched in the contact's name. The phone rang three times before he heard a soft and breathy, "Hello."

"Hi Mom," Noah said. "Thought I'd call and check on you." Okay, it wasn't exactly the truth, but it wasn't a lie, either.

"You all alone without a woman by your side tonight, Noah?" she asked.

"I thought we decided we weren't going to discuss my love life, Mother," he replied sternly.

Elizabeth laughed that wonderful melodical laugh that only she could pull off. "You may have decided that, Noah, but I don't remember agreeing. But the fact of the matter is, I'm right and you know it. So, tell me, why is my handsome baby boy all alone?"

Noah gritted his teeth, already sorry for making the call and trying to find a way out of it, but also in need of someone to talk with. Thankfully he was able to change the subject back around to her, so for the next ten minutes they discussed everything in her life from her latest manicure to the redecorating project that was underway. When he could tell she was tired, Noah said goodnight and that he would talk with her soon.

Mentally drained, he went into the kitchen and poured himself a shot of whiskey. Other than an occasional tequila, Noah Greyson wasn't usually a hard liquor drinker, but tonight he needed something strong, and whiskey was the only choice.

He threw back the amber liquid, letting it burn his throat on the way down and turned off the kitchen light. It was only nine o'clock in the evening, and he was going to bed. Rephrase that. He was going to sleep because there wasn't another damn thing to do.

55
Now

After anything but a restful night's sleep, Noah woke up groggy and with a massive headache. Whether it was from the whiskey or the conversation with his mother, he didn't know, but one thing he knew for certain was that trying to be responsible sucked!

After putting three aspirins in his mouth and chugging orange juice straight from the carton to get them down, Noah took a hot shower and felt better. Cooking was out of the question, so a big bowl of cereal and a pot of coffee was breakfast.

Pop hadn't said what time he would be home, so Noah dressed and got ready to work on his boat. Picking up his phone to check the time, he was surprised to see that he'd missed a call at ten o'clock the night before. The caller ID read Anonymous and that made him smile. The only Anonymous he knew was Stella.

Was it too early to call her back? Or would she already be on the set? While he stood there looking at the screen and trying to decide what to do, Justin Moore started belting out *You Look Like I Need a Drink*, letting him know he had a call coming in. And his smile got bigger when once again, he saw the word Anonymous in the caller ID.

"Good morning, Miss Harper," he said. "Did I miss a call last night?"

"As a matter of fact, you did, N," she teased. "And where were you at ten o'clock? I thought that was just the shank of the evening for you island boys."

He laughed, the day suddenly looking brighter. "Would you believe me if I told you I was in bed?" he asked.

"Oh, I'd believe it; what I'd want to know is who you were in bed with?"

"Are you jealous, Stella?" he quipped and immediately wished he could take the words back. Flirting with Stella Harper was not a great idea, no matter how good it felt.

"I'm going to reserve my right to answer that until a later time," she answered, filling Noah with relief.

"So seriously, what's going on with you this morning?"

"I'm feeling a little nostalgic," she said, and he could almost hear the pout in her voice. "Today's the last day that we're shooting in Miami, and I'm wishing you were here."

The grin he was sporting covered his face, but Noah did his best not to let Stella know how much her words meant to him.

"We had a great time, Stella," he told her. "I'd love to do it again someday. Where's your next gig?"

This time the pout was pronounced enough that Noah heard it and almost felt it. "After this shoot, I'm going home for a while," she said. "It's a command appearance from her highness."

It was the first time he'd heard her really complain about her mother, and Noah didn't know how to respond. He was sure Stella was of legal age so why was she still so tied to her mother's apron strings? It was a question he might need to ask his brother, because one thing was for sure, he wanted no part of pissing off a United States Senator.

They talked for a few more minutes and soon Noah heard Teddy in the background, telling Stella it was time to go.

"You can call me anytime; you know that, right Stella?" Noah said before hanging up the phone.

"Thanks, N," she sighed. "You may wish you hadn't made that offer. Gotta go, bye."

And like that, the feeling of sunshine around him faded into a dark cloud.

56

Now

Once repairs were complete on *The Lark,* Noah started taking out some single day and half day fishing charters and found that it was more enjoyable than he would have thought. He could work around the weather, help Pop at the marina on his open days, and for the first time in years, he and Nick were able to spend time together as brothers and friends.

"So, have you heard from Stella lately?" Nick casually asked one afternoon while they were having a beer on the deck.

"No," Noah answered, his eyebrows raised. "Is there something you're not telling me?" *Like is she involved with someone, or has her mother locked her in a tower somewhere?*

Nick held his hands up. "I haven't heard a word since the night Adam Jennings nearly died, but then, I'm not her confidant anymore. You never have told me what you two did in Miami, other than going shopping together, that is," he smirked.

Noah refused to take the bait. "I watched her work; we had lunch and went shopping, for your wedding present, I might add, but there's nothing else to tell. Stella's different than I thought, though, but in a good way." Of course, he left out the part about the way they blatantly flirted with each other, and the way his body reacted when he saw her in that red bikini, but those things weren't any of his brother's business.

Pop brought them out a plate of cheese and crackers, and the conversation steered away from Stella Harper and on to the upcoming football season. All the members of the Greyson family were big fans of the Tampa Bay Buccaneers, and many memorable Sunday afternoons were still spent in front of the TV, cheering on their favorite team. The conversation ranged from the draft picks to the current quarterback before Nick looked at his watch and said he needed to go.

"I know this change of attitude hasn't been easy for you, Noah," he said, climbing into his Jeep. "I really do admire how committed you are." With a chuckle he added, "Of course you may feel like your nuts are going to explode while you search for the right woman, but hopefully, it'll be worth it in the end."

Noah shot his brother the bird as he watched him drive away. Unfortunately, it was more than his nuts he was concerned about. At that moment, he felt as if his whole body was one big detonator waiting to go off.

He trudged through the yard toward the dock, his mind going a million miles an hour. *How did I get to this place?* he wondered. Yes, he'd let a childhood crush on Lottie escalate to the point where he wouldn't allow himself to care for another girl, but there'd been a few over the years he wished he'd treated differently. The problem was he hadn't, and now those girls were somebody's wife and mother, and here he was, all by himself.

The Lark looked pretty as a picture as she swayed in the afternoon breeze, and he climbed aboard talking to her as he did. "I've really fucked up my life," he told her. "Well both our lives to be honest. I always imagined a woman sitting in the helm with me, laughing as our babies learned to bait a hook. We'd take rides to Coquina Beach and have a picnic in the sand. After tucking the little ones in the cabin when their eyes became too heavy to hold open, we'd throw blankets on the cabin floor and make love, not just have sex. I know, my vision always had curly red hair streaked with gold, but that's where I made my mistake. She was never mine to fantasize about. So, tell me, how do I get our lives back?"

It wasn't that he actually expected *The Lark* to answer, but when a thought came immediately to his head, he thought maybe she had.

"You're right," Noah said out loud. "There isn't any reason why I have to wait for Stella to call me; there isn't any reason at all."

57

Now

After three rings and no answer, Noah was about to give up when Stella answered her phone. "Hello?" she said breathlessly. "Noah are you there?"

"Do I even want to know what you've been doing?" he laughed.

"I was in the weight room and couldn't find my phone," she answered, still trying to catch her breath. "But what's up? It's not like you to call in the middle of the afternoon."

What was up? The part of his anatomy that had been up since he saw her in that red bikini, but he knew that wasn't what she meant. As to why he was calling, that was easier to explain.

"I guess I wanted to hear your voice," he said, and the response was total silence.

Shit! Now I've gone and done it! Said something stupid and...

"Noah Greyson," Stella said, the emotion in her voice raw and real, "that's the nicest thing anyone has ever said to me in my life."

He released the breath he'd been holding inside, and for the first time in several days, he relaxed.

"So tell me, Miss High Metabolism, why are you working out in a weight room, especially on a beautiful sunny afternoon?"

"My mother is announcing her vie for reelection next week, and she's picked out the most godawful dress for me to wear," she told him, and he could almost feel her rolling her eyes. "She's decided that my tits and ass are a little curvier than appropriate, and I'm on a regimen to slim them down."

What! Stella was already rail thin, but he did enjoy her tits and ass, and so did probably every other man in the world. "Did your mom actually says those words to you?" he asked in disbelief.

"Tits and ass? Nope, those are all mine. I'm six feet tall and a size zero, Noah, which is thin even for a runway model. I can't help how mother nature distributed my weight."

"I think you look amazing," he found himself saying. "Speaking on behalf of all red-blooded males, thank God for Mother Nature. But that brings me to a question I'm not sure I have the right to ask. Why do you allow your mother to run all over you like she does?"

Instead of answering, she deflected by asking a question of her own.

"Do you have any special plans for the week after next?" Stella questioned.

"I guess it depends on your definition of special," he joked. "But if you're asking if I have something planned that can't be changed, the answer is no."

"Then meet me in Key West! There's an impromptu celebration at the Hemmingway House, and I was asked to be the hostess. I was going to turn it down, but I'll do it if you'll come be there with me. Please say you will."

Key West *and* Stella Harper? He knew it was a mistake before he opened his mouth, but for some reason, he couldn't tell her no.

"I'll meet you on one condition," he told her firmly. "Tell me why your mother seems to have such a hold on your life."

For a minute she didn't respond but he could hear her crying in the background. "Stella?" he asked. "What's going on?"

"It's because of Adam, Noah," she sobbed. "My mother's holding Adam over my head."

How in the hell do you reply to a comment like that? It wasn't a conversation to have over the phone, that he was sure of, so Noah did his best to alleviate the tension his question had caused.

"I'll come to Key West, Stella," he told her softly. "But we need to have a real conversation about Adam Jennings and this hold your mother has on you; you know that, right? I can't help you or even be a good friend when I'm clueless about what's making you so unhappy."

"Okay," she whimpered. "What if you don't like me once you find out?"

"Nick knows; doesn't he?" Noah said more than asked. "And he's still your friend. Do you think so little of me that you believe I'm less compassionate than my brother?"

"No, but it's…, I don't know, it's different with Nick. I don't have many friends, Noah, not people who like me for me, and I don't want to lose you. Does that make any sense?"

"It makes perfect sense, Stella, and you don't need to worry; our friendship is secure." He replied. "Now give me the information about Key West so that I can make some plans. I've been wanting to hook up with some of the fishing tournaments there and this will be a perfect opportunity. The repairs on *The Lark* are complete; now dish."

Stella gave him the date of the celebration and promised to get back with him once she confirmed her acceptance with the organizers and knew where she was going to be staying.

"Oh!" she exclaimed before hanging-up. "Be sure to bring your best bib and tucker, this is a semi-formal affair."

"My what?" Noah laughed.

"Something besides a pair of shorts and your lavender shirt." Stella giggled. "Although you do look mighty fine in them, but you'll need at least a pair of long pants and a jacket."

"I've been to the Key's before," he answered. "I've always worn shorts. Has the dress code changed?"

"No, silly, but you're going to be my date for the festivities. Now I've got to run so that I can start the ball rolling. Bye, Noah Greyson," she said sweetly and ended the call.

Well son of a bitch! I walked right into that one.

58
Now

The trip to Key West had been easy and uneventful, and Noah was excited when he finally arrived. Two days at sea was nothing, but after his experience in Louisiana, he had to admit that he'd been a little nervous about making the trip.

He maneuvered the fifty-foot Carolina custom into the mooring he'd arranged for, and immediately, a tender was on its way out to meet him. *The Lark* would be his home while he visited with Stella in Key West, and the first thing he needed to do was take care of the financial arrangements and hitch a ride to Pirate Scooter Rentals.

The bright blue scooter beneath him, Noah entered the address of where Stella was staying into his phone's GPS and headed that way. Fifteen minutes later he pulled up to the most magnificent house he'd ever seen. For some reason he thought a villa was a fancy word for condo, but this place was a villa in every sense of the word.

The outside was all a rich, creamy shade of vanilla, sitting on a bluff overlooking the water. Huge windows, covered by white porticos, graced the front, and Noah was certain a swimming pool and tennis court were hiding behind the greenery covered walls of the property. Punching in Stella's name on his phone, Noah stared in amazement while he waited for her to answer.

"There you are!" she said excitedly. "I'm coming out to meet you."

In typical Stella fashion she came bounding out of the house like a two-year-old and threw her arms around his neck. "You're really here!" she squealed. "We're going to have so much fun."

Noah pulled back to take a better look at the girl in his arms and couldn't help but feel a tug at his heart. She had on no make-up, her glossy dark hair was pulled up in some kind of messy topknot, and perspiration glistened off of her flawless skin. A pastel, floral sarong was wrapped around her body from neck to knees so that the only skin visible was her arms and her long-toned calves, yet he'd never been more aroused. At that moment, it was all he could do not to unwind her from the silky cloth and make her his.

"What are you looking at?" Stella questioned when she realized Noah was staring at her.

Without missing a beat, he replied. "Needed to make sure you still have your tits and ass." And they both burst out laughing.

Stella looped her arm through his and led him into the glorious structure, jabbering every step of the way. When he could finally get a word in edgewise, Noah's first questions were about the house. Or rather, *the villa.*

"So, who owns this place, Stella? Please don't tell me some Arab Sheik," he teased.

"Well, I'm not sure if he's Arab or not, but his name is Omar or something like that."

"Are you shitting me?" Noah demanded, running his hand over his face. "A real sheik?"

As soon as he saw the twinkle in Stella's eyes, he knew he'd been had. "Why you little tease," he scolded, grabbing her hand. "What am I going to do with you, Stella Harper?"

The twinkle in her eyes turned sultry, and the temperature in the room seemed to rise by twenty degrees.

"I'll get back to you on that," she taunted. "But right now, let me show you around."

After a tour of the property, which as Noah suspected had an Olympic-sized swimming pool and a tennis court, they stopped in the kitchen where Stella poured them each a large glass of sweet iced tea.

"Seriously, Stella," Noah questioned taking a frosty glass from her hand. "Who owns this beautiful monstrosity?"

"To be honest, I don't know. It's a friend of a friend of my mother's, so that could be anyone from a movie star to foreign royalty, although my guess would be it's some high roller who wants to keep my mom in her senate seat. You never can tell with the Honorable Kathleen Harper."

Noah could hear the unhappiness in her voice when Stella talked about her mom, and even though she owed him a conversation about her mother's hold on her, he knew now wasn't the time.

Instead he casually asked, "And what about your dad, Stella. You never talk about him?"

"Hank? He's okay, as long as he's away from his, "Kitty," as he likes to call her, but I don't want to talk about my parents. Tell me about the newlyweds. Did they like their wedding present?"

Noah let Stella lead him to a covered patio where he told her everything about how Nick and Lottie were doing and how much Lottie had loved the honeymoon decanter. He even shared his disastrous book signing experience which had Stella laughing so hard that she couldn't catch her breath.

When she'd finally calmed down enough to take a sip of her drink, Noah spoke-up. "I've told you about what's been going on in my life; now it's time for you to tell me about yours. I like you Stella, I really do, but I don't understand what's going on between you and your mom." He took her hand and looked directly into her dove gray eyes. "I'm your friend, and I won't turn my back on you, but I need for you to trust me. Can you do that?"

She nodded and wiped away a tear that was beginning to fall.

"It all started when I was seventeen."

59

Then

"Give me one good reason why I can't go!" Stella sobbed into her linen napkin. She knew that getting her father on her side was the only way her mother would agree, which is why she had waited for dinner. It was the one time of day they were all together as a family, and only then, when her mom was home from Washington, like today.

"Stella," her mother said sternly. "You recently signed a modeling contract that any girl in her right mind would kill for. We agreed to allow you to finish out your senior year at Golden Oaks, but attending a high school dance? It's too risky."

"It's my senior prom, Mother," Stella insisted. "Not just some high school dance, and for whom is it too risky? Daddy you understand, don't you?"

Henry Harper coughed, hoping to stay out of the conversation. "Yes, Stella, I understand," he finally said. "But Mommy only has your best interests at heart. Right, Kitty?"

"Of course, it's you I'm thinking of, Stella. On the hill, we're always talking about children today and the freedoms they have. I'm only trying to keep you from making mistakes that might ruin your fledgling modeling career as well as our good name." Kathleen Harper looked as if she was debating a bill on the Senate floor instead of having a discussion with her seventeen-year-old daughter.

"It's Adam Jennings, Mother, you understand that, right? Quarterback of the Golden Oaks football team, captain of the track team; the Adam Jennings who received a full ride to Clemson for both his academic achievements and to play football. He's the most popular boy at school, and he wants to go to the prom with me." Stella was crying in earnest now. "Please, Mother," she begged. "Please let me go.

I don't know that I even want to be a model, but I want to go to the prom with Adam. I know that more than anything."

After what felt like hours of negotiations, because that's what it truly was, Stella was finally given permission to attend her senior prom with Adam Jennings. But with all kinds of stipulations. She agreed to them all; she would have agreed to anything at that moment. All that mattered was she was going to her senior prom, and she was going with Adam Jennings.

The night of the prom was a typical Florida evening in May, pretty much perfect. Stella slipped into her spaghetti-strapped, pink, long floral embellished gown unable to believe that she was really going to her senior prom, and she was going with Adam Jennings! Adam was every teenage girl's dream. With wavy blond hair and steel blue eyes, he had the looks to be a male model and the athletic ability to make it in the NFL. He was tall, broad-shouldered, and beautiful, and for tonight, he was hers.

At six he picked her up in the limousine his parents had rented. After presenting her with a white orchid wrist corsage and posing for numerous pictures taken by Stella's parents, the couple was off to a fancy dinner with some of their classmates.

"Wow!" Adam told her after they were settled in the limo. "You look so hot. This is what you've done to me already," he said, taking her hand and placing it on his crotch. "As great as that dress looks on you, I can't wait to take it off."

Stella blushed, only now forcing herself to remember why Adam had asked her to the prom. Sure, she was beautiful, but so were a lot of other girls in their school. Yes, she had signed a modeling contract, and her mother was a United States Senator, but Stella had something that made her unique. Stella Harper was still a virgin, and she'd promised Adam her virginity in exchange for taking her to the prom.

All through dinner the boys joked about the *after prom* and the hotel rooms they had rented, and the girls laughed right along with them. All but Stella. She loved sitting there with the cool kids and loved knowing she was Adam's date, but in her heart, she'd believed that he wanted to be with her, and he would let her out of their deal. But sitting here listening to him talk with his friends, she knew that her heart had been telling her lies.

Adam was chosen as Prom King, and Connie, one of the other girls who'd gone to dinner with them, was named as Queen. After the crowning, everyone applauded as Adam and Connie were led onto the dance floor for the first dance of the evening. The music was slow and romantic, and even as inexperienced as she was, Stella could see that this wasn't the first time Adam and Connie had been that close to each other and her face burned. Was it envy or regret; she wasn't sure, but she was sure of one thing? This was not how the evening was supposed to go.

She and Adam danced a few times, but never the way he'd danced with Connie. He tried pulling her in tight, but when he did she felt like she couldn't breathe. When he offered her some punch, she drank it down in one gulp, hoping it would cool her off, but it wasn't enough. By glass three, she was giggling as Adam helped her upstairs.

"I need to lay down," Stella told him, the room starting to swirl around her.

"Sure, baby," he said, slipping down the straps of her dress as he lay slobbery kisses on her neck.

"I don't think I like that," she said, wiping at the spot on her neck he'd been kissing. "Please, I need to rest for a minute."

She tried her best to get Adam to leave her alone, but he kept offering her more punch. "If I drink anymore, I'll wet the bed," she giggled, and he immediately put the cup down.

"Look Stella," he told her in frustration. "We had a deal, and now it's time to pay up. Turn around and let me unzip that slinky dress, and you give me what I paid for. You'll get to say you went to the prom with Adam Jennings, and I get your cherry. When I'm a big football star, you can tell your friends all about it. Now turn around."

But instead of turning around she started to cry and that made Adam angry. He had enough alcohol in his system to fuel his flame, and Stella's virginity was how he intended to extinguish it. He grabbed the front of her dress and pulled it down over her strapless bra, leaving Stella shaking and begging him to stop. With one swoop the bra was gone, and Adam's football calloused hands were squeezing and pulling at her tender flesh.

"Please Adam," she begged. "I've changed my mind; please, I want to go home."

158

His only response was to put one of her nipples in his mouth and to bite down. She remembered screaming in pain and Connie barging in the room, demanding that Adam let her go. Stella barely remembered Connie calling her parents and her father coming to pick her up, but the one thing she never forgot was thinking, *My mother was right.*

60

Now

Shell-shocked wasn't a strong enough term to describe how Noah felt. Nick had mentioned an attempted rape, but the story that Stella told him made him feel physically ill. He'd comforted a lot of women, in a lot of different ways, but he'd never been faced with anything like this. Trying to draw from the wisdom of his sister Maya, and the little his brother had shared, Noah pulled the weeping woman into his arms.

"It's okay, Stella," he cooed, stroking her back gently as he did. "I'm so sorry that happened to you and sorry I forced you to tell me, but it's over, and I'm right here."

Stella continued to sob into his shoulder, using Noah's shirt like a handkerchief, as he continued to try to console her. Finally, when she was all cried out, she lifted her head and gave him a weak smile.

"I didn't mean for that to happen," she told him, wiping her eyes with the hem of her sarong. "My Adam file is usually locked tight, but I guess I needed to start at the beginning so that you'd understand."

"Oh Stella," he said, taking her head in his hands and gently pushing a wisp of hair from her face. "What I understand is that you're a strong, amazing woman who ended up in the clutches of a very sick individual. You don't have to tell me anything else, and I promise not to pry again."

"I want to tell you," she answered, her voice getting stronger. "But could we maybe take a break? Teddy went to the market, and I don't want her to come home and find me like this."

"We'll play this however you want, sweetheart, but it's up to you when and where. I won't ask again."

This time the smile she gave him lit up her face. "You called me sweetheart," she said shyly. "I don't think anyone's ever called me that before."

Noah didn't know what he was feeling at that moment other than relief that he had somehow put a smile back on her face. He was sitting with one of the most beautiful women in the world, a two-time Sports Illustrated Swimsuit Edition cover model, and no one had ever called her sweetheart? *What's wrong with this world?*

"Did I see a scooter out front?" Stella asked, totally shifting gears.

"Yeah, I needed something to move around town on."

"Then take me for a ride! I've always wanted a Vespa, but my mom says they're too dangerous. But I'll be safe with you driving." Stella looked so excited that Noah couldn't burst her bubble, but he wasn't sure Senator Harper would feel her daughter was safe riding with him on anything.

"I don't know, Stella," he began, but the beautiful gypsy with a tortured soul was already heading out the door.

"I only have one helmet," Noah said, handing it to Stella. "I want you to wear it. I promise to be careful, but it's the other guy I worry about."

Stella strapped the helmet over her mass of silky locks and sat down behind him on the scooter. "Oh wait," she said first, and proceeded to unwind herself from the floral sarong. Noah thought his eyes would pop out of his head when she stood there in the tiniest hot pink bikini he had ever seen. All the assets Mother Nature had given her were covered as minimally as possible, and when she climbed on behind him, her long legs hugging his thighs, Noah's heart started flip-flopping in his chest.

61

Now

As soon as they took off Noah realized that taking Stella Harper onto the streets of Key West, especially in a hot pink bikini, wasn't a good idea. He knew the lay of the land well enough to keep them away from the normal tourist destinations, and weaving his way through the lush tropical island, they wound up on a strip of beach that was known mostly to the locals.

When Stella climbed off of the scooter, he immediately felt the loss of the warmth of her body and struggled to get control of his thoughts. She'd just told him about the horror Adam Jennings had put her through when she was seventeen, and his heart hurt for her, but it wasn't his heart that was doing the thinking. He had to get *that part* under control.

"There's a food truck!" Stella squealed, as she pulled Noah down the beach. "I've always wanted to eat a shrimp taco from one like they do on *Hawaii Five-O*. Can we Noah, please?"

He wasn't honestly sure that eating from a food truck was the sensible thing to do, but there were other people in line. He crossed his fingers and hoped it was a good decision. After ordering four shrimp tacos and two Mountain Dews, Noah led her to a shady area and sat down in the sand, leaving Stella standing beside him, a petulant look on her face.

"What's wrong?" he asked.

Stella shuffled her feet in the sand, afraid to meet his gaze. "I'm afraid if I sit down, I'll end up with sand and who knows what else in my hoohah," she answered. "There isn't much here covering me."

Noah couldn't keep from laughing although he was in total agreement about not much covering her, and that *not much* was staring him right in the face. Pulling off his shirt, he laid it on the sand beside him, and taking Stella's hand, he gently helped her to sit down in the middle of it.

"You're so gallant, Noah," she praised him, and then surprising them both leaned over and kissed his cheek.

"Whatever," he replied, and handed her a taco to keep from doing something he knew he'd regret.

Stella had eaten her tacos with gusto, telling him over and over again how good they were. He agreed, they were good, but the moans she made every time she took a bite kept him from concentrating on the food. She'd made those same sounds at the restaurant in Miami, and all he could thing about was if she moaned like that eating a taco, think of the sounds she'd make in bed? He was trying to move his mind back to the present when Stella did it for him.

"Did I see key lime pie in that truck?" she asked innocently.

"Seriously, you want pie?" Noah shook his head in amazement. Never in his life had he known a woman to eat so much and still stay so thin.

"Well, I've always wanted to try it, and you know what they say, 'There's no time like the present!'" She batted her long, feathery lashes and there was no way in hell he wasn't getting her that pie.

"Oh, and Noah," she called as he was walking away. "See if they have any unsweetened iced tea. I'm really thirsty, and I'm sure the pie will have more than enough sugar."

Watching and hearing Stella eat the pie was excruciating as she moaned over every morsel and licked the fork clean after each bite. If he didn't know better, Noah would say that she moonlighted as a porn star, but instead, she was a girl who really enjoyed her food. *Really enjoyed it.*

After their impromptu picnic, Noah gathered up all of the trash and disposed of it properly. He'd spent most of his life on and around the beach, and he knew the importance of keeping the sand and the surf safe from human species. He helped Stella fasten the helmet and climbed on the scooter, knowing in a minute he'd feel the heat from her limbs wrapping around him.

"Noah," she said softly, laying her head against his broad back. "Thank you for this. I know there'll be hell to pay when we get back, but I wouldn't trade this memory no matter how much Teddy rants and raves."

She squeezed his waist, leaving Noah to wonder what kind of rants and raves he was in for when he took Stella back to the villa on the hillside.

62

Now

When they pulled up Teddy was sitting in a large rattan rocker under the front entryway; Stella's sarong lying across her lap.

Hardly waiting for the scooter to come to a complete stop, Stella climbed off and handed Noah the helmet. "It looks like I have some damage control to do," she smiled nervously. "I'll call you later, okay?"

Noah put down the kick stand, determined that she wasn't going to face this alone, but Stella stopped him. "I can handle Teddy, Noah; trust me. She may work for my mom, but she loves me, and when push comes to shove, she's always in my corner."

"But Stella, this is wrong on so many levels. You're an adult, and even with all the awful things Adam put you through, it doesn't give your mom the right to run your life like this. I want to talk with Teddy."

"That's sweet, really Noah, but not today," she said as she ran up the walk.

Noah watched the two women go inside and started to put on the helmet Stella had handed him. He wasn't sure what the fragrance was that he was smelling, something citrus and floral all mixed together. One thing he knew for certain, it was the scent of Stella, and he liked it.

After stocking up on supplies for the next few days, Noah decided to go for a swim. It was hot and muggy outside, and his afternoon with Stella had left him with more unanswered questions. There was nothing like pushing your body through the Florida surf to bring clarity to your mind. He and Nick had been doing it since they were kids, and while they were both excellent swimmers, Noah only wanted to swim for pleasure, unlike his brother who thrived on the competition.

The tender once again picked him up from the mooring where *The Lark* was anchored, and Noah buckled a bag with a beach towel and a bottle of water onto the back of the scooter. He chuckled, thinking about Stella and her reluctance to sit directly on the sand, and grew warm thinking about how close his face had been to that tiny scrap of pink and her long lean body. He was in deep trouble where Stella Harper was concerned, and he hoped the waves of the Key West waters would help him figure out what to do.

The swim was amazing, and even though he returned to the scooter with no resolution to his feelings for Stella, his heart was quiet for a change, and his body was exhausted. Back on *The Lark,* he rinsed off the saltwater and threw on a clean pair of shorts and a T-shirt. He decided that an easy dinner at the Tiki Hut by the marina and a good night's sleep was what he needed to be back to normal.

By ten o'clock, Noah still hadn't heard from Stella, but he kept telling himself she said she'd call, just not when. She'd shared some horrible things with him today, and maybe she felt embarrassed or unsure of herself. Or maybe Teddy had really done a number on her, but whatever it was, he wouldn't know until they could talk. He climbed into his berth, hoping the gentle rock of the waves would lull him into a peaceful slumber, but an hour later he was still wide awake.

This must be how a girl feels when a guy says he'll call her, Noah thought. All those times he'd used that line without any intention of calling was making him feel like crap, and that's what he was thinking about when the cloud of sleep finally washed over him.

63
Now

The sun coming up over the water was always a spectacular event. Especially if you had a front row seat from the deck of a boat. Noah sipped his coffee as the streaks of pink and orchid slashed across the morning sky, planning his day as the colors put on a light show.

Appointments were scheduled with the organizers of fishing tournaments in late January and mid-March, and he felt good about both of them. His buddy from Louisiana had put in a good word for him, and that was major when a new boatowner wanted to be considered to enter a team. Now all he needed was to enjoy his day in Key West, and that was going to start with breakfast.

It was a short walk to the restaurant where he'd had dinner the evening before. He'd seen a scrambled eggs and shrimp dish advertised and wanted to give it a try. Deep in thought, he paid no attention to the sleek black limousine sitting by the pier when he climbed out of the tender, but no sooner had he stepped foot on land than he heard his name being called.

A tall, well-dressed woman who looked vaguely familiar climbed out of the limo and moved in his direction. "Mr. Greyson," she said formally.

Noah was dressed in dark board shirts, a long-sleeved Anna Maria Island T-shirt, and flipflops. His hair needed cut, and he hadn't shaved in a couple of days, giving him more of a rogue look than he would have liked when he met Stella's mother, but apparently, that's what he was about to do.

"That's me," he replied, refusing to give in to her apparent intimidation. "Can I help you with something?"

Senator Kathleen Harper looked him up and down, a slight smirk on her face, but Noah's eyes met hers and matched her glare for glare.

"Do you know who I am?" she questioned.

He knew alright but the last thing he was going to do was give her the upper hand, so he fibbed a little. "No ma'am," he grinned. "I don't believe I do."

The Senator huffed a little under her breath before replying, "I'm Senator Kathleen Harper," she spouted indignantly. "Stella's mother." And then, as if it was the most important thing in the world she threw in, "Surely you're a registered voter."

"I am a registered voter Senator Harper; I just may be registered for the other party. That being said, it's a pleasure to meet you. What brings you to the wharf at this time of day?"

"You really are nothing like your brother, are you?" she questioned.

"Look, we started off on the wrong foot," Noah said, not wanting to make things worse for his friend. "I'm sure you're in town to see Stella, and I think that's great. Why you're down here at the crack of dawn questioning me isn't so great. If there's something you need or something that I can do for you, please let me know. If not, it's time for breakfast."

"What are your intentions towards my daughter?" she asked pointedly.

Noah smiled. "That's easy," he answered. "I intend to be her friend. Is that what you want to know?"

"What I'm asking is do you think because my daughter is young and wealthy you can talk her into some kind of tawdry love affair and then blackmail her for money? Because if you do, you have another thing coming." Senator Harper had her arms crossed in front of her, and Noah swore he could see smoke coming out of her nostrils.

Noah was fuming now too, but as calmly as possible he replied. "Have some respect for your daughter's intelligence, lady, and as for my feelings toward Stella, they're none of your damn business."

Noah walked away knowing that he may have just made the biggest mistake of his life, but he wasn't going to let Stella's mother push him around, and if he could stop it, she wasn't going to push Stella around much longer either.

There was so much acid churning in his stomach that there was no way he could eat, and as soon as the limo pulled away, Noah found a shade tree, sat down, and pulled out his phone.

As soon as he heard the voice on the other end he said, "I need some help, big brother. I think I just fucked up."

64

Now

"I thought we had this talk," Nick told Noah after hearing about his brother's meeting with Kathleen Harper. "You seriously do not want to be on that woman's bad side."

"The way you make her sound, she's like a member of the mafia, Nick. Surely she wouldn't have needed your help protecting Stella if that was the case."

"Not mafia, Noah," Nick laughed. "But she has a good strong case of entitlement. Kathleen was a model herself in her younger days and then married a mogul in Henry Harper. Add her Senate seat to that and you have a powerful woman used to having things go her way."

"So, what's the hold she has over Stella, Nick? She started telling me about her prom ordeal yesterday, but she became so emotional she couldn't go on. Adam Jennings is the villain here, right? What can the Senator be holding over Stella's head?"

Nick could hear the frustration in his brother's voice. "Noah, I promised Stella that her story was safe with me remember? I'm not going to bale on that promise, even for you. But one thing I can tell you is this. Adam Jennings made a big mistake, and Stella's mother compounded it. I tried to get Stella to realize that she was the victim in all this, but her mother knows how to manipulate her, and she does."

"Shit Nick, it's all so wrong. Stella's the nicest girl in the world, but her mother is a piece of work. And what's the story on Teddy? She acts more like a keeper than a manager."

Nick chuckled. "You have it bad, don't you, brother?" he asked.

"You're out of your mind, Nick," Noah spat. "She's a sweet kid, and I'm trying to be a stand-up guy for a change; that's all."

"Have you seen her in a bikini yet?" Nick taunted. "Because once you do, all thoughts of Stella Harper being a sweet kid will go right out the window."

"Bite me!" Noah said sharply. "Every person on the planet has seen Stella in a bikini, haven't they? She's graced the cover of Sport Illustrated twice, not to mention all those women's magazine covers she's been on, and anyway, I thought you didn't have any ulterior motives where she was concerned."

"Calm down, Noah," Nick chuckled. "It's been three years since I was on Stella detail, and she wasn't much more than a teenager. I never thought of her as anything more than a girl in need of help, but that doesn't mean I didn't enjoy the perks of the job."

When he hung up Noah kicked the sand in front of him, realizing that he hadn't received any real advice from his brother. He felt like he was thirteen again and about ready to attend his first boy/girl party. He remembered like it was yesterday asking Nick what he should do and never getting a straight answer. It wasn't until years later that Nick finally confessed that he couldn't give Noah any advice, because at that point, he didn't have any real experience with a girl either.

As it turned out Noah became the Greyson brother who figured out the way around girls and kissing, but he would have gladly changed all that if Lottie would have looked at him like she did Nick.

65

Then

"Sarah Roberts invited me to her birthday party on Friday night," Noah told his brother one day after school.

"Cool," Nick replied. "Her brother Aaron's in my class, and he's a good guy."

Noah's face became red as he tried to find the way to ask his brother about making out. He'd heard through the eighth-grade grapevine that Sarah wanted to do that with him, and he was scared to death.

"Remember when we were kids and I used to ask you about kissing Lottie?" Noah started.

"We're still kids, Noah," Nick laughed. "But yes, I remember. What makes you bring that up now?"

"Well, I've heard that Sarah wants to make out with me at the party, and I don't know how. I don't want to look like a fool Nick; she's really pretty."

Noah was so into his fear of making a mistake that he didn't notice Nick trying to avoid a direct answer.

"Kissing isn't something I can teach you, Noah; it's just instinctive. Either you're good at it or you're not."

Nick walked out of the room leaving Noah without the answer he was looking for. But it turned out he was right. When the time came, Noah knew exactly what to do, and he was good at it. Very good as a matter of fact.

66

Now

After a ride up and down Duval Street and taking selfies at the Southern Most Point in the United States Buoy, Noah was edgy and bored. He stopped into Jimmy Buffett's famous Margaritaville restaurant for a Cheeseburger in Paradise and a cold Landshark. While they were both excellent, he would have been happier eating tacos out of the back of a food truck with Stella. When the waitress came by to remind him to leave room for a piece of their famous key lime pie, he asked for the check. It was like adding insult to injury.

He checked his phone at least a half a dozen times to make sure that he hadn't missed a text and finally knew he had to man up. His first thought was to storm the villa and demand to find out what was going on, but thankfully, he went with his second which was to send Stella a text.

> *Hey Stella. I haven't heard from you and just wanted to make sure all is well. Mommy dearest doesn't have you locked in your room, does she? That was a joke, but I guess she's told you about our talk, and anyway, I didn't handle it too well.*
> *Call me, okay? N*

As soon as he hit send, he wished he could take it all back, but that was the trouble with texts. He stood by the scooter for about five minutes waiting for bubbles to appear, but when they didn't, he muttered, "Screw this," and took off. He had things he needed to do, and there was no time to waste.

By the time Noah got back to *The Lark,* it was early evening and there was still no word from Stella. Not wanting to mess with the tender again, he grabbed a cold can of Coors Light out of the cooler and stretched out on the deck.

Reggae music was being played at the Tiki Hut; the sky was a mixture of azure and opal; and he was lounging on the deck of his boat, a cold brew in his hand. Everything was perfect with the world except one thing; he still hadn't heard back from Stella.

In his entire life, Noah Greyson had never chased after a woman. He'd known since the party at Sarah Robert's that girls liked him, and that knowledge had given him an edge. But this was different, right? He was concerned about Stella and his conversation with her mother, and the last thing he wanted was to hurt her more than she'd already been hurt. But chasing after her? No, that wasn't it at all.

He had just popped the top of his second beer when the ping of an incoming message sounded. In his haste to grab the phone, his beer toppled to the floor, and Noah slipped in the golden liquid puddling on the deck.

"Shit!" he yelled, as he pulled himself up. His shorts were soaked, his beer was wasted, and his pride was injured, but none of that mattered when he read the text.

> *Sorry, N, I've been at the Hemmingway House all day making final arrangements for tomorrow night and couldn't return your call. You met my mother? She didn't say a word. Hmmm, not sure if that's good or bad.*
>
> *Anyway, gotta run. The event starts at 7 tomorrow night. Give your name at the door. Can't wait to see you in your bib and tucker!* ☺ *Stella*

67
Now

The next day was productive as Noah met with the fishing tournament coordinators and was accepted for both the January and March events. They would even hook him up with a team of seasoned fishermen and a couple of deck hands. All he had to do was pay the entry fee and have his boat ready with equipment and bait.

There were still several hours to kill before he needed to start dressing for the evening's festivities, so Noah drove the scooter back to Duval Street and decided to do some sightseeing. First stop was the Mel Fisher Maritime Museum.

As he walked through the museum and watched the film, Noah remembered Pop telling him about the great treasurer hunter Mel Fisher and his almost lifelong hunt for the Atocha, the Spanish galleon sunk in 1622. Noah was mesmerized by the pictures and artifacts and even purchased a book and an Admiral Gardner coin to take home to Pop.

After that, he stopped at Sloppy Joe's Bar for an order of Conch fritters and Arepas—grilled Columbian cornbread stuffed with mozzarella cheese—and washed them down with a Sloppy Joe's Island Ale. Again, he was offered key lime pie, and again, he refused.

When the waitress handed him the check, Noah noticed a braided silver bracelet hugging her wrist, and he realized he wanted to give something special to Stella to celebrate their friendship. He paid his tab and went in search of the perfect gift.

There were several jewelry stores in Key West to choose from, and he scoured each one. Would she like a necklace or bracelet, silver or gold, freshwater pearls or turquoise? When he passed a beautiful display of rings, a saleswoman offered to help him, but just thinking about buying any type of ring for a woman had him breaking out in a sweat.

Noah had never bought a piece of jewelry for a woman, even his sister Maya, but this was something he wanted to do. He was determined to buy the perfect thing, but what that was he wasn't sure. He looked over every display and peeked in every case, the saleswoman following his every step when suddenly, something caught his eye.

A delicate golden charm of a mermaid wrapped around an anchor, a bale attaching it to a fine Figaro chain caused Noah to stop in his tracks. It seemed so appropriate that he said, "I'll take it," before he thought to ask the price.

Turns out that 18K gold was considered a luxury purchase, but Noah didn't care. The necklace represented both of them, and it was the gift he wanted to give his friend Stella Harper. He handed over his credit card without another thought and waited while the clerk rang up his purchase.

He left the store with a smile on his face and a spring in his step; all the while, his heart was pounding. He'd dropped a boatload of money on a woman, and he wasn't sure what it meant for their relationship or even if he wanted it to mean something. But he was certain of one thing, the necklace would look incredible draped around Stella's slender throat, and he couldn't wait to give it to her.

Knowing that riding around Key West on a scooter with an expensive piece of jewelry in his pocket wasn't a smart idea, Noah headed back to the boat. It had been an eventful day, and he had enough time to relax on the deck of *The Lark* before getting ready for the evening's gala.

Once the tender had dropped him off, he took the necklace out of the box so he could admire it again. The clerk had offered to wrap it for him, but he had a vision of Stella lifting her mane of inky hair while he fastened the clasp around her neck. He was a little lost in that fantasy when it hit him. *What if she doesn't like it?* He remembered a sign at the store stating that all sales were final so if Stella didn't like his gift, he was in a world of hurt.

He grabbed a can of Coke out of the cooler, kicked off his sandals, and stretched out on the sectional, the necklace still in his hand. The soft drink was cold and helped against the heat of the late afternoon sun, even though what he really wanted was a couple beers. But Stella's big event was in less than two hours, and tonight he needed to make a better impression on her mother. So, he stuck with Coke and thought about the situation at hand. He was a commercial charter boat captain, and Stella was the supermodel daughter of a United States Senator and a finance mogul. No matter how he spun it around in his head, he couldn't find a happy ending for the two of them.

68

Now

"It's now or never," Noah said out loud, starting up the scooter. In hindsight, he realized that he should have called a cab or an Uber to take him to the Hemmingway House, but it was too late for that now. He strapped the helmet around his chin, checked his inside pocket to make sure Stella's necklace was safe, and pulled out of the harbor and into the Key West sunset.

Noah had done his homework on Hemmingway. The last thing he wanted was to embarrass Stella in front of her celebrated guests, but when he pulled up to the beautiful old Spanish style home, he had to admit that he was impressed. The Hemmingway House was nestled in the heart of Old Town Key West and had been the home to one of America's most celebrated authors for over a decade. Tonight, it glittered with thousands of tiny lights strung around the property, giving it a beautiful ethereal elegance.

He waved away the valet and parked the scooter himself, as far away from the luxury cars as possible. Taking a big gulp of the warm night air, Noah straightened his tie, ran his hand through his thick dirty blond hair and thought, *you are so out of your element here, Greyson.* But he had a date with a gorgeous woman, and nothing in the world could have stopped him from keeping it.

A light melody was coming from strategically placed hidden speakers, and people were scattered about drinking champagne and making small talk. Noah felt as if every eye was on him as he ascended the walk and gave his name to the woman at the front door.

"Noah Greyson," he told her. "I'm a guest of Miss Harper."

And like magic he looked up and coming down the stairs was his mermaid. The one who had been inhabiting his dream the night Stella had come to the marina looking for Nick and the one deep in his pocket that he planned to give to her later. She was dressed in a long, sparkly emerald green skirt that hugged her curves and cascaded down her long, lanky legs. Her top was iridescent and so shear you could almost see through it, but her dark shiny tresses hung down in waves, covering all but her midriff.

For the first time in his life Noah Greyson was speechless. And when the goddess standing in front of him put her arms around him and whispered in his ear, "I like your bib and tucker; you look good, Captain Greyson," he almost lost it. His body responded by going from hot too hard in an instant. Who was this vixen, and what had she done with Stella?

Just then Senator Harper and her husband entered the room, and Stella moved away.

"Mr. Greyson," Senator Harper said extending her hand as she looked him over from head to toe, "You're more like your brother than I gave you credit for."

He nodded, thankful for the hundred bucks he'd dropped on a decent haircut and shave, and for the gray Armani suit he'd purchased for Nick and Lottie's wedding. He may have been only a commercial charter boat captain, but that didn't mean he couldn't look appropriate, did it?

A passing waiter offered him a glass of champagne, and he lifted it in a toast. "To Stella," he said. "The belle of the ball."

Stella blushed and her mother bristled, and Noah noticed the look of jealousy in Senator Harper's eyes. *It must be really hard,* he thought, *for a power seeker like Kathleen Harper to relinquish attention to her young, beautiful daughter.* But he wasn't here for Stella's mother, and he was determined not to let Stella down.

Couples were starting to dance so Noah sat down his glass of champagne and offered his hand to the amazing woman in green. "May I have this dance?" he asked, pulling Stella into his arms. He could tell by the look of amazement on her face that she wasn't used to upstaging her mother.

He led her onto the dance floor, mesmerized by the dazzling smile he saw on her beautiful face.

"You're a pretty good dancer for a fisherman," she teased. "You really do look extremely handsome tonight. I have to say though, I kind of miss your scruffy pirate look, although obviously my mother prefers this GQ thing you have going on."

Noah gave her a twirl that had her laughing out loud. "Don't ever underestimate me, sweetheart."

"You did it again," Stella said softly. "You called me sweetheart."

His heart pounded and his stomach did somersaults as the music and dance ended. "Can we go someplace a little more private?" he asked, his voice husky and unsure.

Stella nodded and grinned as she led him through the crowd of people to the back entrance. The moonlight shimmered over the pool, and even though a few couples were enjoying the warm Florida evening, they were able to find a secluded spot underneath a tall winding banyan tree.

69

Now

Noah couldn't remember the last time he'd been this nervous with a woman. Normally he knew exactly what to say and exactly what to do, but this time was different. This was Stella, his friend whose life he still didn't have a good handle on, other than knowing her mother was a barracuda. He ran his fingers over the charm in his pocket, wanting so badly for it to mean as much to her as it did to him. He cleared his throat a couple of times before speaking.

"Stella," he finally said. "I'm glad that we've become friends, and I hope you know how much I respect you and like being around you. The last few months have been really special and well, I wanted to give you something tangible to let you know that I'm always here for you."

Slowly he pulled the necklace from his pants pocket and gently laid it in her hand.

"Oh Noah!" she squealed, examining the mermaid draped across the anchor.

The tears were rolling down her cheeks as she handed him back the necklace.

"It's perfect, and I love it!" she exclaimed. "Will you put it on me?" she asked, turning around.

It was his vision coming true, and his hands were shaking as he lifted the cascading waves of hair away from her neck. For a moment he stopped, thinking how it would feel to kiss the soft porcelain skin before him, but he snapped out of his daze when she turned her head his way.

"Everything okay?" she questioned with a smile.

"Just having a hard time with the clasp," he fibbed, and he gently placed the chain against her collarbone and fastened it.

"Well, what do you think?" she asked when she turned back to face him.

"I think it looks beautiful. You look beautiful," he answered. "Maybe we need to go inside so you can see for yourself."

Stella stroked the charm, reminding him of how Lottie caressed the locket from her gran, and it hit him how much alike the two women were. They were both vulnerable, yet strong, both with issues from high school that had clouded their futures, both gorgeous, inside and out, and above all else they were his friends.

Stella slowly stepped his way, her hand never letting go of the charm and gave him a soft kiss on the lips. "This is the most wonderful gift I've ever received," she said, her eyes still damp with tears. "I'll never forget this night, and I'll never forget you, but I have something I want to say."

Noah didn't move a muscle, scared to death of what she wanted to tell him. Did she think they were hanging out too much; was her mother pressuring her to remove him from her life? The silence while he waited for her to speak was driving him crazy. When she did, he thought his heart would stop.

"I want you to make love to me, Noah".

There was noise all around them, yet the silence between them was deafening. Noah saw the fear and confusion in Stella's eyes as he searched for the words, the right words to say to her without making a mess of everything.

"Stella," he began, clumsily taking her shaking hands into his own.

But she refused to let him go on. "Please, Noah," she pleaded. "Just hear me out."

He nodded, trying to concentrate on her stormy gray eyes instead of the knot in his stomach. Her long feathery lashes were laced with tears, and he could tell she was trying to hold them back.

"I like you Noah Greyson," she told him. Giving a small smile she added, "And I think you like me."

"I do like you, Stella," he interrupted. "That's why—"

She put a finger to his lips and shook her head, "No talking."

"I'm almost twenty-four years old," she continued. "I'm ready to have a real life. I've lived in a cocoon of my own making, because I allowed my mother to hold Adam over my head, but I'm ready to emerge. I want to spread my wings, Noah, but I need you to teach me how. I want my first time to be with someone I trust and who I know won't just use me."

Had he really heard right? "Your first time?" he demanded. "You mean to tell me you've never had sex, Stella? You're the most sought-after girl in the world. How can that be?"

"I told you in Miami that I hadn't been on a date since my senior prom," she answered. "What did you think I meant?"

"I don't know; honestly, I don't know," he replied, running his hand through his hair. "But Stella, this is serious. You don't just hop into bed with someone because you're tired of being a virgin. You're first time needs to be special and with someone who really cares about you."

"And you don't, is that it?" Her lips were quivering now as she spoke.

"No, it's not that at all. I do care about you. That's why I'm not going to be a part of something I know you'll regret later."

Stella's cheeks were burning with shame when she looked at him. "I'm sorry if I made you uncomfortable," she said softly, trying not to cry. "I guess my mother's right, I'm not very smart where picking men is concerned. Please forget that I said anything."

She turned her back to walk away, but Noah took hold of her wrist and pulled her back towards him. Without giving himself time to think, his lips crushed against hers in a kiss so deep and passionate that it left them both gasping for air. Tipping her face, he placed soft kisses on her eyelids and nose as he worked his way back to her mouth. This kiss started out gentle, but the heat between them was so intense and raw that Noah pulled back, afraid that he was losing control.

"Stella," he said, laying his forehead against hers. "I don't want to be another bad choice in your life. I'm not sure I'm up for the responsibility you're asking of me, but if you had any doubts about my feelings for you, or how badly I want you, you need to think again. But we're going to take this thing slow so that no one ends up being hurt."

She nodded her head, the blush creeping up over her face made her seem more innocent and alluring. But before she could respond, a voice came from around the corner.

"Here you are, Stella," Henry Harper said to his daughter, totally ignoring Noah. "Mommy's been looking everyplace for you. It's time for the unveiling."

He turned his daughter towards the house and marched her towards the door as if she was five. Self-control had never been his strong suit, but for Stella's sake, he kept his mouth shut and followed them inside.

71

Now

What the hell just happened? They'd been having an intimate conversation when abruptly she was led away like a lamb to the slaughter. Noah's thoughts were all over the place, but he knew he needed to get a handle on the situation and his emotions. One minute he was fastening the gold necklace around her neck, and the next she was admitting that she was still a virgin. But it was the kisses, and the promise of more that really had him confused. How could she have walked away with her father after that?

Sprinting to the house, all he could think of was that they weren't done talking, and he had to move Stella away from her parents so they could continue. But when he reached the house, he saw her standing in the middle of the room, smiling and talking as the guests circled around her as if nothing had happened between them. When the room erupted in applause, Noah moved in her direction only to see a parent standing on each side, her mother's armed entwined with hers.

"Mr. Greyson," Senator Harper said very arrogantly. "Wasn't Stella's presentation lovely? She's been such a great ambassador for literacy in our state."

Noah had no idea what the Senator was talking about, and he hadn't heard enough of the speech to discuss it, so he nodded and looked Stella's way. The music had started back up, and he hoped asking her to dance again would be a good way to get her away from the glowering stare of her mother, but he was wrong.

"Oh, there you are Donald," the Senator said, grabbing the hand of a distinguished looking man of about fifty. "I know how much Stella has been looking forward to meeting you, and what better way than through a dance."

Noah was furious but did his best not to let Stella's mother see how angry he was. He was pissed off at the Senator's antics and determined to remind Stella of her vow to no longer allow her mother to control her life. He looked at his beautiful friend, but she turned away as if she couldn't look him in the eye.

Noah was seething inside as he watched his beautiful mermaid moving around the dance floor in the arms of another man. And when the guy stroked the skin of her smooth strong back and dipped his hand almost dangerously low, he grabbed a glass of champagne from a passing waiter and downed it in one drink. The Senator turned away, totally dismissing him, leaving Noah alone without a clue as to what was going on.

He was deep in thought when he heard the Senator talking. "They make a handsome couple, don't you think?" she said with a haughty tone to her voice. "Stella's father and I both feel an older man would give her the firm hand that she needs. She's such a flighty girl you know."

What in the world was wrong with these people? They were talking about their daughter like she was chattel in medieval England. Finally, not able to stand it any longer, Noah strode on to the dance floor and pulled Stella from the arms of Donald, whoever the fuck he was.

"Excuse me," he said forcefully to Stella's dance partner as he slipped his arm around her waist.

"Wait just a moment," the man said, adjusting his tie and lifting his head like a bull moose trying to intimidate another male. But it wasn't working on Noah.

"Stella," he said, trying to gain control of the situation. "What's happening here?

"That man is Donald Richardson, and he's the owner of the villa where we're staying," she answered quietly. "That's all I know except you need to back down. If you cause a scene or embarrass my mother, the outcome won't be good for either one of us."

The look she was giving him was one of a scared lost girl and not the woman he had shared one of the most meaningful kisses of his life with, and it was breaking his heart.

"I'm not leaving you, Stella," Noah told her. "I'm your friend and I promised you could always count on me."

"Stella Kathleen, we have other guests," her mother said stepping between them. "Now go apologize to Donald and then mingle. You're here as the hostess for the gala, not to be fawning over a fisherman." She strung the last word out for impact, and her meaning wasn't lost on him.

Stella caressed her necklace and gave Noah a weak smile. "My mom's right, Noah," she told him. "I'm on duty tonight, but I'll call you tomorrow. Thank you so much for coming and for my wonderful gift; I'll always treasure it."

And then with one small spark of defiance she leaned over and kissed his cheek before walking away.

He'd never felt so helpless in his life. His first instinct was to look for the waiter with the champagne and take the whole tray, but he knew that over drinking wasn't the answer. Especially when he had to maneuver his way back to *The Lark* on a scooter. So, he stood there watching and waiting, but for what, he had no idea.

Finally, he knew that the magic from earlier in the evening was gone, and it was time for him to accept it. Looking up he saw Stella gazing his way, her hand holding tightly to the gold shimmering against her throat. He gave her a half-hearted smile and mock salute goodbye and walked away.

72
Now

By the time he made it back, the anger was gone but the hurt had set in. While he waited for a tender, Noah went to the Tiki Hut and had a double shot of tequila. He had just finished sucking on the lime when a hot to trot beach bunny sat down beside him.

"You look like you're all dressed up with no place to go," she purred in his ear.

Noah barely looked in her direction. A band aid might cover the wound he was feeling tonight, but he wasn't interested. He shook his head, placed a wad of cash on the bar, and went outside to wait for his ride.

The Lark felt cold and lonely when he stepped inside. Loosening his tie, he opened the fridge looking for something to fill the empty spot in his gut. *Could this night have been a bigger shitshow?* he wondered. Finding an old wedge of cheese, he ate around the spots that were dried out and hard and threw the rest in the trash. He popped the top on a can of Coors and wondered if it was a bad idea to drink beer on top of tequila and champagne, but he chugged the frothy liquid anyway.

His phone had been ominously silent all evening, but he checked his messages to be sure before placing the call that needed to be made. As soon as he heard a, "Hello," his tirade began.

"They're crazy, Nick, you know that, right?" Noah half yelled. "You tried to warn me, but I wouldn't listen and now they've pulled me into their little fucked-up life. Crazy, rich people that's what they are, and I don't do crazy."

Nick chuckled on the other end. "It sounds to me like you've been hitting the sauce little brother, how much have you had to drink, and please tell me you're safely tucked in for the night."

"Considering the night I've had, I'm nowhere near done drinking, but I'm in for the night, so you don't need to worry. I just turned down a chance with a beautiful woman, Nick, and all because of those crazy fucking Harpers. I swear there's something evil going on there, I think you need to investigate them."

Nick couldn't stop laughing as he continued to listen to his brother spew obscenities about the Harpers, which only made Noah yell more. When he was finally quiet, Nick spoke.

"I don't know what happened to you tonight, Noah," he said. "But this is a conversation for tomorrow. You need a bottle of water and three aspirin and to call me in the morning. But not too early because it's Saturday. And yeah, the Harpers are a little crazy, but Stella's worth the headache. Anyway, I'm pretty sure you think she is, and that's what matters."

Noah listened to his brother's words, and because it was true that he did think Stella was worth it and that he had drunk more than he should have, he blurted out, "Do you know she's still a virgin, Nick? She's the most fucking gorgeous woman in the world, and she's still a virgin."

Nick sighed. "I guess I didn't know the status at this point in her life, but I knew back when Adam was stalking her. But she was barely twenty and had lived through hell, so it made sense. Now forget about the Harpers and go to bed. We'll talk in the morning and see if things look brighter."

"Nick," Noah said before hanging up the phone. "Thanks for always being there."

"I always will be," Nick answered. "Now I have to get to sleep before Charlotte starts to snore. This is one of the aspects of her pregnancy I'm not enjoying."

That was enough to bring a smile to Noah's face, but he still cracked open another beer.

"Are there aspects you do enjoy?" he quizzed.

Nick chuckled. "I hope someday you find out. But for now, quit drinking, and call me in the morning."

73

Now

The sky was spilling in around the blinds when Noah opened his eyes. *Where in the hell was the sound of that snare drum coming from,* he thought, pulling the pillow over his head. But the more awake he became he realized it was coming from inside his head.

"Ahhh," he groaned as he tried to sit up. Hands holding the sides of his head to stop the ceaseless pounding, he cautiously put his legs over the side of the bed and made his best attempt to stand. Between the rocking of the boat and his still blurry vision, Noah felt the bile in his throat threatening to unleash and barely made it to the head in time.

The face looking back at him in the mirror was cringeworthy to say the least. Red, bloodshot eyes, hair sticking up every which way, and a yellow pallor to his skin gave him the appearance of a zombie. Noah splashed his face with the tepid water from the pump, and using his hands for a cup, slurped down just enough to swallow three aspirins. He made a face as the bitter taste of the pills started to dissolve in his mouth and then went in search of coffee.

The small coffee pot in the galley was bubbling away. It was times like these he wished for one of those fancy machines like Lottie had, where all you did was put in a pod and pull out a hot cup of joe. Thinking about Lottie made him remember that he needed to call Nick, but searching for his phone seemed like too much effort.

The first sip of the piping hot brew scalded his tongue, and Noah swore, but by the time he was into his second cup, he began to feel normal. Or close to it anyway.

Beer cans littered the cabin, bringing back the memory of the night before. It had all started out so well. How in the hell did it all get out of hand like it had?

After a third cup of coffee and a shower, Noah was finally convinced that he'd live. He hadn't been on a bender like this since his college days, and here at this moment, he swore he'd never go on another one.

"I'm too old for this," he said out loud and picked up his phone to call his brother.

"Well good morning, sleepyhead," Nick chuckled. "Although its eleven-forty-five so it's almost afternoon."

"I'm not up for the quips Nick," Noah grumbled. "I called so that you can tell me what to do, because I honestly don't have a clue."

"Last night you kept saying the Harper's were crazy. Maybe you need to tell me what happened so that I'm at least up to speed on their latest tricks."

Noah told Nick everything except the part where Stella had asked him to make love to her. He decided that was too private to share with anyone, even his trusted big brother.

"So now you see why I say they're crazy, right?" Noah asked. "I was supposed to be Stella's date, and they practically married her off to that old geezer right in front of me. That's why I have to know what the hold is Senator Harper has over her daughter. I mean it Nick; this is serious."

"Okay, but only because Stella already told you the hard part. Grab a cold drink, Noah, because what I'm going to tell you will definitely heat you up." Nick blew out a big breath and began telling his brother the ending to the story of Stella Harper's prom night.

"As you can imagine, when Stella finally got home, she was mortified to face her mother, and her mom did nothing to alleviate her daughter's misery. In fact, instead of consoling and soothing her like a normal mother would, she berated Stella, telling her over and over that it was her own fault. Then at eleven o'clock at night, she forced her already traumatized daughter to undergo a physical examination to make sure she hadn't truly been raped even though Stella told them over and over that she hadn't been. It was the Senator's way of showing her daughter that she was still in control, knowing that Stella would be totally humiliated. It was after that when Stella totally shutdown."

"The bitch!" Noah yelled, smacking his hand against the chair where he was sitting.

"Pretty much," Nick agreed and continued the story. "Stella was sent to bed, still with no comforting, and her mother told her that a chaperone would be hired by morning to travel around with her and make sure she didn't cause any more embarrassing situations. She also said that for everyone's sake, since there hadn't been an actual rape, they weren't going to press charges against Adam Jennings because the whole thing was Stella's fault to begin with, and none of them needed the publicity."

"And where was her dad all this time, Nick? Doesn't the man ever have the balls to stand up to his wife?"

"Apparently not. Anyway, Stella wasn't allowed to return to school or graduate with her class, and by the end of the week, Teddy was a permanent fixture in her life."

Noah swore under his breath. "I still don't understand," he said. "Stella says everything is her fault and she can't let Adam die without forgiving her. Does her mother have her that brainwashed?"

"No, but this is where the really ugly part comes in. Senator Harper didn't press charges against Adam. She didn't want the media to know, but she wanted revenge and she did something worse. I'm sure Stella told you about Adam's dream to play in the NFL, and how he had a full-ride scholarship to play football at Clemson? Well, Kathleen called an old friend who's on the board of regents and had Adam's scholarship revoked. I'm not sure how they did it, but it devastated the kid and pretty much killed his dream."

"Are you expecting me to feel sorry for the little shit, because I've got to tell you that I don't." Noah was fuming mad now and thankful for the cold drink.

"I understand, Noah. I don't feel sorry for him either," Nick said. "But when Adam lost it and started stalking Stella, her mom never missed an opportunity to remind her that it was all her fault. That's a heavy weight for a young girl to carry, especially when her career took off and she catapulted to the top rung of the modeling ladder.

"I don't know what to say," Noah replied. "Adam Jennings had a problem before Stella came into his life; that's obvious. And let me guess. She wants to apologize for what her mother did by having his scholarship revoked, right?"

"That's what I'd say," Nick told him. "She never said that to me, so it must be something she decided after he shot me and was sent to a maximum-security prison. I personally don't feel like she owes him a thing, but Stella's a much better person than I am."

"She's special Nick, but you know that. Now help me figure out how to get her out from under the clutches of the Wicked Witch of the West, because that's the only thing that's going to save her."

74
Now

Unfortunately, you can't save someone who doesn't want to be saved. By four o'clock, and no word from Stella, Noah sent her a text.

You said you'd call Stella. What's going on?

He wasn't sure that he'd hear back, but almost immediately, his phone dinged.

Sorry, Noah, I've been really busy today. Was her only reply.

He was dumbfounded. *She'd been really busy?* What kind of lame-ass excuse was that? Should he text her back? Call? He was totally lost as to what to do when the music started, signaling an incoming call.

"Stella!" he exclaimed into the phone. "Thank God, I've been worried sick."

"I didn't mean to worry you, but I've had a lot to think about." He could almost see the anguish on her face as she spoke.

"And just what have you been thinking about?" Noah questioned, a sinking feeling erupting in his stomach.

"You know, about our conversation and everything. But the thing is," she said, obviously struggling to go on. "I think I was a little carried away by the romantic atmosphere last night, and to be honest Noah, I'm not up to someone with your, um, skills."

He gripped the phone, trying to calm himself down before for responding.

"My skills?" he asked her. "And what skills would those be, Stella? Obviously not my conversational ones because if I recall, it was you who asked me to take you to bed."

"Noah, please," she pleaded. "Don't make this any harder than it already is. Friends sleeping together really isn't a good idea, and I'm sorry that I asked that of you."

He dragged his hand over the stubble on his chin and said, "Is this you speaking, Stella, or some ploy of your mother's to get me out of your life? Because I'm honest when I tell you, I don't fucking understand what's going on."

He thought he heard her crying, but there was no way in hell he was letting her off the hook that easily. Maybe she was having regrets for their conversation the night before, and maybe she was scared, but in his soul, he believed it was something more, much more.

"I'm going back to Tampa with my parents and taking a little time off work. I think that's what I need to piece my life together. Anyway, I can't tell you enough how much I appreciate everything you've done for me. You've been the best friend I've ever had, Noah Greyson, the very best friend."

Her sobbing was deeper now, and it was like a punch to Noah's heart. "Stella," he said softly. "Please tell me that you aren't going to let your parents marry you off to that old man, and please tell me that you haven't let him touch you."

"You don't have to worry on either count, Noah," she told him. "I made it perfectly clear to Donald that I wasn't interested in anything. He left the party with some woman and didn't even stay at the villa last night."

"Are we still friends?" he asked, afraid to hear the answer.

"Of course we're friends," she answered. "We're just not going to be friends with benefits."

Noah sighed, not sure if their talk had made him feel better or worse. Finally, he told her, "It's too late for me to leave tonight, but I'm going to head out at first light. Be safe, Stella Harper; you know where to find me if you need anything."

He didn't even wait for her to say goodbye, just ended the call. His head hurt, his stomach hurt, and his heart hurt, so he figured why not? If he was going to suffer the trifecta from the loss of a woman, the least he could do was do it in a place with loud music and booze.

The Tiki Hut was swarming with early evening drinkers when Noah sat down at the bar and ordered a beer and a plate of wings. Across the room he saw the woman from the night before looking his direction and quickly turned away. The way he was feeling, the last thing he wanted was to hook up with a strange woman.

195

The wings were okay, but not great, and after the first swig of beer he remembered the hangover he'd awakened with, so he set it aside and asked for a Coke. It was a beautiful evening, and couples were strolling on the beach when a sandy haired co-ed walked by and a memory hit him as if it was yesterday.

He'd told Stella the night before that your first time needed to be with someone that you cared about, someone who was special to you, but it hadn't started out that way for him. His relationship with Molly O'Brien, the first girl he'd ever slept with, the *older woman* in his life who helped him become a man, had defiantly been memorable. Until now, all these years later, he hadn't realized how special it had been.

75

Then

"Next to AMI, the Outer Banks is my favorite place to be," Jake O'Brien told Noah excitedly. "We go every summer, but this is the first time my folks have ever let me bring a friend."

The two boys were sitting in the backseat of the Lincoln Navigator, each with a Nintendo DS portable gaming system in their hands. Jake's parents, both veterinarians in Sarasota, were riding in the front seat, making their own plans for the two-week vacation and allowing the boys to make theirs.

Pine Island, where the O'Brien's rented a house every summer, was about a fourteen-hour drive from Anna Maria Island, so Noah had spent the night with the family because they wanted to be on the road early the next morning. He was both excited and terrified, but since he was only a few weeks away from turning sixteen, he worked towards excited with each passing mile.

"Where does your family go on vacation?" Jake asked casually.

"I don't think we do," Noah responded. "My pop's awfully busy in the summer so we stick around and help out at the marina. When we lived in New York with our mom, she took us to Atlantic City once, but I was too young to remember much about it."

"No vacation? Man, that would suck, but you're going to like it on the island. There's so much to do."

Noah was having trouble understanding how one island could be that much different from another, but he was anxious to find out. Jake was one of his best friends from school, and they always had fun together, but secretly, Noah wished that he was taking this adventure with his family. For some reason, having Pop, Maya, and Nick with him always made things better.

It was close to dark by the time they arrived at the beach house which, as it turned out, was a monstrosity on the sound side of the island. Noah helped the family unload the SUV, and then they drove into town for pizza.

"We always have pizza our first night here," Jake's father told him. "After that, it's all the seafood you can eat! You do like seafood, don't you?" Dr. O'Brien asked him.

Noah nodded but again wondered, *how is this different than AMI?*

The boys had a bunk room on the bottom level of the house, and after returning from dinner, they settled in. Next to them was a game room with a big TV and pool and fuse ball tables, and for the first time, Noah decided that this island might have something to offer him that Anna Maria Island didn't.

The next day Jake's parents were up and out early to do what they came to do; take care of the horses that still roamed the uninhabited areas of Pine Island. Noah was eager to see the horses running free, and the O'Brien's promised him that before they left he would.

He and Jake spent the morning exploring the neighborhood and took a four-wheel excursion through the dunes in the afternoon. There was a pool and a hot tub at the house, and for two teenage boys left to their own devices, it felt like heaven. At least for one day.

By evening Jake was complaining of a headache, so they stayed in and grilled hamburgers. Just before Jake's mom was about to call them to the table, the front door opened and a female voice yelled, "I'm here; where is everyone?"

Noah watched intently as the girl behind the voice entered the kitchen, giving hugs and kisses to Jake's parents before turning his way.

"So, you're Jake's little vacation buddy," she said with a cocky grin. "What's your name?"

He thought she was beautiful. Her long sandy brown hair was tied in a ribbon at the nape of her neck, and even though they weren't close enough for him to see her eyes, he guessed the color was green, or maybe hazel. It was too hard to tell. She was about average height and slender but with enough curves to definitely fill out the cut off jean shorts and tank top she was wearing.

"I'm Noah Greyson," he said, trying his best not to stammer.

"Well, Noah Greyson, it's nice to meet you, I'm Jakes's sister, Molly." Turning towards her mother, she said, "I'm starving; is dinner ready?"

All throughout dinner, Noah listened to every word Molly said and watched as she told her parents all about her life at the University of North Carolina. Her face sparkled when she spoke about how happy she was about changing her major to drama, and he felt certain she'd be a star someday. Jake, it turned out, didn't feel well enough to eat and sprawled out in a big recliner, watching TV while the rest of them enjoyed hamburgers and corn on the cob.

After dinner, Jake's dad handed Molly some cash and told her to go to the local ice cream hangout for a half gallon of peach. "And take Noah with you," he told her. "He's probably going stir crazy."

Molly drove an old, yellow Volkswagen convertible with a black ragtop that she called "*Bee.*" Noah had to put the seat all the way back to squeeze his tall frame inside, and when he finally buckled in, he saw she was staring at him.

"What?" he asked.

"I was just wondering if you've ever kissed a girl."

"Of course I have," he smirked.

"Well what else have you done?"

Was this for real? Was this pretty college girl flirting with him or just giving him a hard time?

"I've done stuff," he answered, and the thinking about that stuff had his jeans feeling a little uncomfortable.

"How old are you, Noah Greyson?" she asked as they were backing out the drive.

"I'll be sixteen in a few weeks," he told her, trying to keep the embarrassment off his face.

Molly smiled and started the car, driving towards town. Noah saw the entrance for the *Cone*, but she drove right past it, turning instead into a secluded strip of beach. Once *Bee* was far enough off the rode not to be seen, she turned off the engine and took Noah's hand.

"Have you ever done this?" she asked, placing his hand on her breast.

"Sure," he said, trying to act braver than he felt.

Slipping his hand under her tank top and onto the skin above her lacy bra, she once again asked, "How about this?"

Noah didn't know what to do. Sherry Barnes had let him undo her bra and cup her breasts, but then she'd made him stop. Is that what Molly had in mind, too?

"Yeah, I've done that, too," he told her, his voice becoming huskier with each question.

"But you've never gone all the way, right?"

He wanted to lie and tell her he had experience, but instead, he told her the truth. "No, I've never gone all the way."

Molly reached up and pulled his mouth to hers, but Noah was an experienced kisser and quickly took control. The kiss was tentative at first, but then he brought it deeper and stronger. She arched her back against his hand and moaned when he slipped it down far enough to take her nipple between his thumb and forefinger. When Molly finally pulled back from the kiss and looked Noah in the eye, he saw desire and fear but not regret.

When they finally arrived home with the ice cream, Molly went to her room and Noah watched TV with Jake and his parents. His thoughts were all over the place, but he was thankful for the big bowl of frozen custard sitting in his lap and the sex talk he'd had with Pop about protecting himself as well as a partner. He wasn't sure if anything more would happen with Molly, but he was prepared if it did.

As it turned out, Jake had some kind of weird virus and spent most of his vacation resting, which gave Noah and Molly lots of time to be together without arousing suspicion. Molly wasn't afraid to show Noah what she liked, and he was an eager student, and in those two weeks he learned a lot about how to please a woman.

On the last night before she was to head back to Chapel Hill, and Noah and the O'Briens were leaving for AMI, he and Molly climbed the dunes behind the house one last time, holding a blanket and bottle of beer and each other's hands. The stars were bright, and the sky was clear as Noah spread the blanket over the sand. There was so much he wanted to say to her, but he couldn't get out the words. Instead, he gave her a long, slow kiss and helped her out of her shorts and halter top.

When it was over, he gently kissed her and wondered how he would ever be able to say goodbye. They talked about staying in touch, even seeing each other over Molly's Thanksgiving and Christmas breaks, but they both knew that would never really happen.

"This has been the best vacation of my life," Molly told him wistfully.

"Mine too," Noah laughed. "But then, it's pretty much the only one I've ever had."

Molly rolled her eyes, and Noah took her hand in his. "I have a question I need to ask you," he told her.

Oh…kkay," she stammered, seemingly nervous about what the question might be.

"How old are you, Molly O'Brien?" he grinned.

She let go of his hand and gave him once last kiss. "I'll be twenty in a few weeks," she smiled and walked right out of his life.

He thought of Molly every day for months, and slowly, she became a remembrance of the summer he turned sixteen, and the time he went from being a boy on the cusp of adulthood to the time he became a man.

76

Now

"Can I get you anything else?" the bartender asked.

"Huh?" He'd been so deep in thought that it took Noah a minute to remember where he was. "I mean no, just the check, please."

His thoughts were on Molly O'Brien. He hadn't seen her since the night of his and Jake's high school graduation. He'd wanted to talk to her, but she was with a man, and he had been afraid it would be awkward. Instead he had nodded and smiled, and she did the same. That was over ten years ago, and he hadn't thought much of her since, but tonight, watching the pretty, sandy-haired girl on the beach, he was filled with memories and wistfulness.

Noah called the scooter rental company and arranged for them to come pick up his ride from the past few days. While he waited to turn over the keys, he ran his hand over the smooth leather seat, recalling how it had felt to have Stella sitting behind him, her thighs tightly hugging his hips. That day had held so much promise; how had it all gone so wrong?

The tender dropped him off for the last time, and Noah gave the guy a good tip, thanking him for the great service. Now that his headache was gone and there was some food in his stomach, he was forced to deal with the remnants of his pity party from the night before. Empty beer cans were strewn about the cabin, and his sleeping quarters were a mess. Finding a trash bag, he began picking up the empty cans, apologizing to *The Lark* as he went.

It was dark by the time everything was back in shape. He wanted a beer but settled, instead, for a can of lemonade left in the fridge by one of his nieces. It didn't have a lot of flavor, but it was cold and wet, and that's all he really needed.

Noah took the drink and a bag of chips to the deck and got comfortable. It was a beautiful evening, and the stars were glowing like a million tiny candles lighting the sky. All he wanted was to watch them without thinking about women. Fat chance.

"I'm not cut out for forever," he told the glimmering constellations. "I've tried and I've failed, and I need to move on. The longest I've ever been with a girl is the two weeks with Molly, and can that even be called a relationship? It was good; I'll say that for it. No, it was great, but it was nothing more than growing pains for both of us. Then the time with Sissy that was over before it really ever began and then Stella. She really got to me, but I was a putz, and I'm tired of that feeling."

He took a drink and rolled up the chip bag and went inside. Tomorrow was a new day, and he had a long trip ahead of him. He was headed home, once again taking with him a bruised heart and a broken ego.

77

Now

Pop was standing on the dock, a cold beer in his hand when Noah pulled in. After *The Lark* was secure and Noah was standing beside him, he smiled.

"This feels like déjà vu all over again," he joked, handing Noah the beer.

"It feels like hell all over again, if you ask me," Noah grumbled. "You've been talking to Nick, haven't you?"

"He's worried about you, son; hell, we all are. What can I do to help?"

Noah couldn't help but grin. "You already did, Pop," he answered, putting his arm around his dad's shoulders. "No matter how bad life is out in the big old world, it's always brighter when I come home. Now tell me, what did you fix for my homecoming dinner?"

"You're not returning home from war," Pop laughed. "Only a few days on a beautiful island with a gorgeous woman. But come to think of it, maybe you were at war after all."

"I'll admit, I do feel like I've been in a battle, but one of wits not weapons. Senator Harper is one crazy broad, and she's doing her best to make Stella crazy, too. But it doesn't matter, I'm over the whole whacko family."

"Are you sure about that, Noah?" Pop asked.

"That's what I'm going with so let's get back to dinner. Do I need to go pick something up?"

"Well actually, dinner's being catered in tonight. Nick and Lottie will be here in about an hour, and she's bringing beef stew and homemade bread," Pop told him. "You have time to shower and unpack, though."

"Look," Noah said, scrubbing his hands over his face. "I appreciate that you and Nick think I need some kind of intervention, but really, I'm okay. What I need is a nice quiet evening and a good night's sleep."

"I hate to break it to you, Noah," Pop said sharply. "But not everything's about you. Thanksgiving is in two weeks, and we need to make plans."

It wasn't often that Pop raised his voice to any of his kids, but when he did, they knew they'd gone too far.

"I'm sorry, Pop," Noah said, genuinely remorseful that he'd been such a jerk. "I'm anxious to try Lottie's cooking, and it will be great to be with family tonight, really."

"You know this family has a lot to be thankful for this year. Nick recovered, he and Lottie are married, and I'm going to be grandfather again. I want a big old-fashioned Thanksgiving with the people I love. Is that too much to ask for?"

Noah smirked and asked, "And will Shelly be part of that celebration?"

"Wise-assed kids," Pop grumbled, but as he walked away added, "the answer is yes. Shelly is most defiantly part of what I'm thankful for."

78
Now

Thanksgiving ended up taking place at Stavros' in Tarpon Springs, and despite Pop and Charlotte's planning, Dimi insisted on doing the cooking. His family joined the Greyson clan, and it truly was a big old-fashioned Thanksgiving celebration, with a mixture of both Greek and American favorites. Shelly was there too, of course, and it made Noah smile to see the look of happiness written across his dad's face.

With the big commercial dishwasher running, and the food packed away, everyone went to Maya and Dimi's house to watch football. It was as much a Greyson family tradition as turkey, but for some reason, Noah was too restless to focus. When everyone cheered, and he realized he didn't have a clue why, he snuck away unnoticed and went outside.

"Hi, Socs," he said, scratching the big fluffy golden ball of fur behind the ears. "I'm sorry I didn't sneak you out a turkey leg, but come to think of it, that's probably for the best. Maybe that fancy poodle down the street would be a better option, right? Although if I know my sister, she's taking care of your urges for the ladies."

Socs gave his best impression of a smile, happy to have someone's attention.

Noah heard his name called and turned towards the voice of the woman he had once thought of as his one true love.

"Lottie," he said. "Why aren't you and the beach ball in watching the game?"

"I'm glad to see you didn't lose your sense of humor along with your appetite," she laughed, cradling her belly. "I could ask you the same question. You didn't eat much, and that's not like the Noah Greyson I know and love. Are you okay?"

"I'm okay," he finally said. "But okay isn't enough anymore. I feel like I'm at a crossroads and don't know which way to turn."

"Is this about Stella?" she questioned.

"Some of it. I haven't talked to her since Key West, and I'm concerned for her. I've tried to be a good friend, but it doesn't seem to be enough."

"Could it be that maybe you want more than friendship and she doesn't?"

"I wish I had the answer to that Lottie, I really do," he said. "To be honest, I don't know what either one of us wants, and that's part of the problem."

"So maybe you two need to talk? I don't know what happened, and it really isn't any of my business. Unless you want to waste the next twelve years of your life questioning your every move, kind of like your brother and I did, you'll call her."

"You're sounding like a parent already, Lottie," he teased. "I think you're going to be a great mom and one thing's for certain, pregnancy becomes you."

She blushed at the words but smiled at his sincerity. "I admit, it's grown on me," she said, a soft glow on her face. "But don't tell your brother. He's already talking about the next little Greyson, and I just want to make sure I'm good at this one before signing up for more."

"You'll be great, I have no doubt, and guess what? I feel better than I have all week. So, you think I need to call her; is that what you're saying?"

"It is Thanksgiving," she grinned. "Wishing her a happy holiday just seems like good manners to me."

"Thanks, Lottie," Noah beamed. "I'm going to call her right now."

Noah took the phone out of his pocket, but before he could punch in a name, he saw a new text message, and when he read it, his world stood still.

Hey sailor, I'm ready for that drink. Give me a call. Sierra.

Prologue
Knot For Love

Noah stepped out of the gangway at the Louis Armstrong New Orleans International Airport with sweaty palms and a racing heart. He hadn't seen Sissy in months, and even though they'd spoken several times since Thanksgiving, he was nervous about seeing her again. He never had gotten around to calling Stella that day, and he had no idea what this visit really meant for him. Right now, he was what his Pop would call *being between a rock and a hard place.*

She said she'd meet him at his gate in the Southwest terminal, but apparently a hundred other people had made that same commitment. He used his height to his advantage as he scanned the faces in the crowd, and just like the waters parting, the people moved out of the way, and there she stood. Sierra.

A snug, turquoise blue dress hugged her curves, ending inches above her knees, showing off her smooth shapely legs. Some kind of sexy strappy boots adorned her feet and ankles, and her light brown curls hung freely around her shoulders. What caught his attention and was obvious to every man in the place, was that she wasn't wearing a bra as her firm, ripe breasts strained against the material trying to contain them. But it was her smile, and that deliciously pouty mouth that had Noah weak at the knees.

"Wow," he smiled, pulling her in for a hug. "What have you done with Sissy? You know the girl who served me shrimp and grits back at The Bait Bucket?"

"She's still there," she quipped, placing her hand into his. "But we're in New Orleans now, and what you get is Sierra. Is that a problem?"

The fragrance of freshly picked apples was radiating from her hair as Noah leaned in for a gentle kiss. "Actually, I see it as a solution," he grinned, using his free hand to pull her in closer.

"And what's it a solution to?" she teased.

"I'll show you later," he winked and gave her the kiss they'd both been waiting for.

Acknowledgments

An author comes up with an idea, but no book is ever complete without the guidance and help of others. I call Barbara Dena the beta reader to the stars! She came into my life at a time when I was questioning my writing and soon went from my beta reader to my friend. I can't thank her enough for her support, and her ability to see things in my words that I don't always see myself.

B.B. Swann is a Twitter friend who asked me to read the ARC of her YA Romance, *Breaking the Barriers.* I enjoyed it so much that I knew right away that I wanted to include it in *Noah's Lark.* Thank you, Bonnie, for both a lovely book about teenage love and interracial relationships, and for allowing me to present it at the Book Nook!

Coming up with a cover design for this book was a challenge. My publisher, Terri Gerrell of Southern Yellow Pine Publishing, convinced me to try a cover with an actual person on it, as opposed to a graphic like we used on the AMI Series. I had a very definite vision of what Noah Greyson should look like, and a very definite vision of what I wanted in a cover, and graphic designer, Gina Davis, delivered both. She and Terri spent long hours trying to put together just the right design, and I'm more than grateful.

How to you begin to thank, and acknowledge, an author of the caliber of Jerri Hines, for enthusiastically agreeing to read your book, and giving feedback on it? Jerri is the author of beautifully written historical romances, and the fact that she took the time to read *Noah's Lark* means the world to me. From the bottom of my heart, thank you.

And of course, I have to acknowledge and thank my faithful readers. Nothing brightens my day like a message on Facebook asking when the next book will be available. I'm a wife and mom who became a banker and turned her love of reading into a new career as an author. Without all of you, my Fairytale would never have come true. Thank you, I love you all.

Until we read again…

Blessings,
Dana L.

Follow Dana to hear the latest.

Website: DanaLBrownBooks.com

Facebook: @DanaLBrownAuthor

Twitter: @DanaLBrownBooks

Instagram: @dana_brown_author

Email:info@danalbrownbooks.com

Amazon Author page:amazon.com/author/danalbrown

CPSIA information can be obtained
at www.ICGtesting.com
Printed in the USA
LVHW051539260423
745367LV00001B/87